WARRIOR AWAKENED

ODINSHIELD BERSERKERS BOOK 1

AVERY HAYNES

Pieridae Press

Print ISBN: 978-1-7379713-0-6

eBook ASIN: B08WWTNT6L

For mom,
thank you for being my biggest cheerleader and making such
amazing cherry torts

Odin's men went to battle without armor and acted like mad dogs or wolves. They bit into their shields and were as strong as bears or bulls. They killed men, but neither fire nor iron harmed them. This madness is called berserker-fury.

— *YNGLINGA SAGA* BY SNORRI STURLUSON

CHAPTER 1

*E*rich Birkeland woke with the taste of another man's blood in his mouth. The salty, coppery tang coated his tongue and the savory taste trickled down his throat. It took a couple of blinks to clear his eyes and he took a quick inventory of his surroundings. Nighttime. Dark alley. A diesel engine passed the mouth of the alley. A woman and a man argued somewhere nearby. Triton City, Sardova. His adopted home town.

With a groan, he sat up and worked his jaw from side to side. It was sore, but nothing to worry about. The same couldn't be said for his side. He lifted his shirt to investigate. A long jagged cut, most likely from a serrated blade, stretched from his back to his abs.

Erich took in the scene around him and let out a low curse. Bodies lay crumbled before him in various grotesque poses. Definitely some broken bones amongst them. One of them moaned. Rage grew within him at the sound. This time a normal human-type rage, not the beastly rage that he had spent the last seven years successfully suppressing.

Until tonight, that is.

1

He considered ending them right then and there, but stopped himself. Despite their attempts to conceal their identities, the fact that some of them were still alive could mean only one thing: they were supernatural. Supes didn't die easily.

Hissing at the sharp pain in his side, he rose to his feet and leaned over the body closest to him. Like the rest of them, the man was fit and heavily muscled. Dark stubble dusted the lower half of his face and his dirty hair lay in thick ropes around his head. Erich grunted. He couldn't recall much of what had happened, but he did remember that this one had been the toughest fighter of them all and had been the last to go down. The facial hair and general scrubbiness of him screamed shifter, but something was off.

Erich surveyed the four other guys scattered around the alley. They were dressed like shitty, drunken lumberjacks, practically announcing themselves as shifters, wolf shifters to be exact. It was too much, though. They fit the stereotype too well.

As he looked back down, the man's tattoo caught his eye, peeking out from what was left of his torn shirt sleeve. Erich hitched up the raggedy sleeve to reveal the Sign of the Bear. He frowned. Not a shifter. A berserker from the Frelshednar clan.

If they had been shifters, trying to kill him would have made sense. He had spent a solid couple of years ridding the city of criminal supernaturals. Payback is to be expected. But a berserker? This one had the intricate tattoo that signaled allegiance to the Frelshednar, a group of berserkers who refused to follow the laws set forth by the Head Council and instead allowed their inner beast to rule them.

Erich frowned. The two berserker clans had been at odds with each other for decades, but they had always maintained the tenuous agreement that bloodshed between berserkers was the ultimate crime. That was the one rule that the Frelshednar had agreed to follow. No killing another berserker. Sure, there had been a couple of fights here and there, but nothing like this. As he took in the scene in front of him, he knew, without a doubt, that these men had been trying to kill him.

A siren rang in the distance. His knee throbbed. Somewhere, in one of the apartments above him, a child was crying. The blood of his enemy danced along his tongue.

The beast inside of him wanted to roar in victory, but Erich refrained. He wasn't a beast anymore.

He stood over the man who had attacked him. He wanted to crush his throat underneath the bottom of his boot. Just casually place it against the thick neck and press down until he felt flesh give way and bone snap. The perfect time would be now. He should kill these men who dared to try to kill him. The muscles in his leg twitched. They were eager to seek revenge.

Years of study and meditation stopped him. He was Ulfhednar. He was more than the beast within him. As much as he wanted to finish what they had foolishly started, he didn't want the wrath of the North to bear down on him. He needed their support. An attack on him was an act of war, and this was a battle he wouldn't be able to fight alone. He fished his cell phone out of his pocket and sent a quick text.

Deep voices sounded nearby. The men spoke softly, as if they didn't want to be overheard. Erich cursed again. He had wasted valuable time fantasizing about revenge. A pointless endeavor that might cost him his life.

Moving silently across the alley, he pressed himself against the wall so he was partially hidden in shadow. It wasn't ideal, but it'd have to do. The men grew closer, snippets of conversation reaching his ears.

"—do it tonight. Otherwise, he'll—"

"I know—said to meet him—"

Erich calmed his breathing. From the sounds of their footsteps, there were only two of them. After sending five supes to kill him, why would they only send two to follow up?

As they came into view, he grabbed the jacket of the man closest to him and yanked him off balance. The man let out a shriek.

Something was off.

At the last moment, Erich eased up and just pushed him against the wall instead of slamming him through it. Holding him with his forearm, he turned to glare at his partner, who was holding his hands up in front of him, his face as white as a sheet.

"Stay cool, man," the second guy said. "We don't want any trouble."

Erich turned back to the man under his arm. Raw terror covered his face as he grabbed at Erich's arm. He smelled of fear.

Humans.

Erich released him and allowed the man to drop the few feet to the ground. The man coughed and scurried away from him, toward the perceived safety of his friend.

"Leave."

The men didn't hesitate. With fearful glances back at him, they ran down the street.

Erich took a deep breath and slowly let it out. His blood hummed with the thought of battle. His beast hungered for more. He ignored it. There would be no more bloodshed tonight.

Without another glance at the contorted mess of bodies littering the ground, he stumbled out of the alley. Clutching his torn jacket in front of him to cover the blood on his shirt, he made his way to his apartment, careful to remain in the shadows. His knee throbbed with each step and the pain in his side was an annoying, continuous burn.

A woman walked toward him. She gave him furtive glances as she clutched her tote bag close to her side and crossed the street. Erich took stock of his movements. The last thing he needed was to look like someone who had just killed and maimed a bunch of people.

Drawing a deep breath, he straightened his shoulders. His neck cracked and popped like he had been holding it in an unnatural position for too long. His knee screamed at him as he forced himself to put his entire weight on his leg and walk normally.

When his apartment building came into view, he quickened his pace. Going up the few steps to the outer door was a challenge, but he gritted his teeth and managed it. Taking the stairs to his second-floor apartment was out of the question, so he hobbled over to the elevator. Although it was late, the building was very much awake. Music thumped out of an apartment nearby. Two men were laughing down the hall.

After he turned off the security alarm in his apartment, he took stock of the main living area. It was spotless. A good sign that the place was empty. Nia never left the apartment without picking up the place. Something about not wanting to be embarrassed if she died and people had to come to pack up her stuff. Pretty morbid. His eyes flicked to Nia's room. Pitch black.

He made a beeline to his bedroom. Taking off his ruined shirt, he cursed the Frelshednar again for their stupidity. He was a man of few possessions and they had ripped his favorite shirt. He balled it up and threw it in the corner. It didn't matter now. Deep in the back of his mind, he knew what he had to do. Where he was going, he didn't need fancy shirts. But first, a shower.

Despite the amount of blood on his hands and clothes, he

was still shocked when he saw his reflection in the mirror. Dried blood had left rust-colored streaks around his mouth and had coated the front of his neck. His hair was wild, stiff, and darkened by blood, but his eyes sparkled as if such perversity excited him.

Erich showered until the water flowing down the drain turned from red to clear. Then he soaped up again, trying to scrub the effects of what he had done from his memory. Fuzzy details from the fight were coming back to him, and he didn't like what he was remembering. The thrill of the battle, the joy as another man's blood splashed against his skin, the elation as the light faded from his attackers' eyes excited him, making it hard to breathe.

With a curse, he turned the knob to the left, gritting his teeth against the increased heat of the water. He lifted his head and allowed the scalding water to slam into his face, welcoming the pain as it cleansed him of the effects of his berserker rage.

Despite his anger toward the Frelshednar, a part of him rejoiced. His blood was pumping and his body was thirsty for more, even enjoying the scalding water that was supposed to be his cleansing. He was torn between anger and euphoria and his mind felt tangled as he tried to get a grip on it.

It had been almost a decade since he'd had a good brawl. Oh, he'd spent many rounds fighting in the octagon, taking his boredom out on whatever unsuspecting human was dumb enough to challenge him. But he was always in control and pulled back so as not to damage his opponent. There was never any risk of him losing or being hurt. This was different. For the first time in seven years, he had felt like his life was in danger.

And it had felt fucking fantastic.

"Fuck!" he yelled, a release of both despair and jubilation.

He turned off the water, wrapped a towel around his waist, and headed into his room to get dressed. He dug deep into the back of his closet and pulled his steel-toed boots out of his old duffel bag. Despite his promise to never go back, he hadn't been able to bring himself to throw them away. It had been years since he'd worn them, but as soon as he pulled them on, the familiar feeling of home washed over him.

He quickly tossed a few things into his duffel. They would be here soon and he might as well be ready for them.

CHAPTER 2

*D*r. Sadie Carmichael gave an involuntary shiver as she entered the cool depths of the county morgue. She definitely preferred the living over the cold, stiff bodies of those who had passed.

It didn't help that the victim she was going to see might have been murdered under circumstances that hit a little too close to home.

Detective Rosa Santiago was waiting for her, her characteristic leather jacket tossed casually over her shoulder and her black, curly hair tumbling loosely down her back. As usual, she was calm and collected with only the slight tension around her eyes revealing any clue that something was bothering her.

"Detective Santiago, thank you for waiting for me."

Rosa shrugged and headed into the viewing room. "No problem. This isn't my case, but as soon as I saw the cause of death, I knew this was more in your lane."

She was right. Supernatural deaths were way too big for the Triton police department to handle. Most humans didn't even know supernaturals existed, let alone the fact that some insisted on wreaking havoc. After the Blood War ended, the Great Hunt had pushed most supernaturals underground in fear of being hunted and murdered. Even after a thousand years, only a few select humans were let in on the secret, and that was only because some circumstances required it.

Sadie followed Rosa to a linen-covered table in the back of the room and pulled back the sheet. The sight of the pale young man on the table was heartbreaking. Sadie picked up his records. Just like the first victim, he had been drained of most of his blood. The only signs of trauma, besides the gaping wound at his throat, were defensive wounds and bruises where it looked like the perpetrator had held him in place during his assault. Sadie placed the file back on the table.

"He was drained, just like the other one," she said.

"Yes," Rosa said. "And besides the obvious wound at his neck, the coroner reported bruising at his wrists and needle marks on his arms."

"Drug abuse?"

Rosa shrugged. "Most likely," she said. "And there's this." She lifted his left arm to reveal the underside of his wrist. Sadie's stomach dropped at the familiar floral tattoo.

"He's an alara," she said, her voice barely above a whisper.

Rosa nodded grimly. "Yes. I suspect the first one was, too, though she didn't have a tattoo." Sadie suddenly felt light-headed and leaned against the table for support. The room grew unbearably warm, like someone had turned on a heat lamp and pointed it directly at her. With shaking hands, she took off her jacket and placed it on the empty table next to her.

"Why do you think the first one was an alara?"

"Little things that her friends and family said during interviews. She always gave the best advice when someone felt sick. She gave the best massages that would help any sore muscle. Things like that. No tattoo though."

Sadie ran her finger along the delicate design of the victim's tattoo. It perfectly matched her own. While the alara did not belong to an official organization, they loosely held to the same beliefs. Respect for others. Respect for the land. Never harm another.

At some point, centuries ago, they had adopted the intricate floral design as their symbol. "Brother, may your soul find peace amongst the Mother," she whispered.

Rosa stared at the body, her face thoughtful. "Could this have been your people?" she asked, her voice soft.

Sadie suppressed a shudder. Her people. It was true that she had been born into The Children of Light, but as soon as her healing powers revealed themselves, she had become something to be confined and consumed. She hadn't spoken to her parents or anyone of the Children in over a decade.

"They never cut this deep," she said, shaking her head. "They have blood rituals, but nothing that leads to death. Not anymore."

"Maybe they've escalated."

Sadie couldn't dispute that point. By the time she and her sister had managed to escape, the whole group had been in a frenzy about the upcoming Era of Light. It was possible that their offerings may have grown deadlier.

Rosa cleared her throat. "We've contacted all known members of The Children of Light. They all have pretty solid alibis."

"Let me guess, they all happened to be in assembly during the time of death."

"Yes. Do you doubt them?"

Sadie sighed, her gaze lingering on the poor man in front of her. Man? He was practically a boy, just entering manhood. Just a few years younger than her sister. To have his life snuffed away all because of some crazy group's ritual was beyond tragic. "I don't know. Things tended to occur at the spur of the moment. So it's possible that they just happened to have assembly during that time. But they wouldn't think twice about lying to enforcement if it meant protecting themselves."

"I suspected the same."

Sadie turned away. An alara was dead. The similarity of the victims and cause of death pointed to a serial killer. Or a crazed cult that fed off of the goddess-given powers of young, vulnerable alara. Either way, her boss needed to hear about this.

"Was there blood at the crime scene?" Sadie asked.

"Nope. The blood was gone, just like the other one."

Sadie shuddered, consciously aware of her own blood flowing through her veins. She thought of the two alara victims. What did it feel like to have their blood drained from your bodies? What were their last thoughts? Did they think of their families? Were they too afraid to think of anything at all? Rosa stepped into her field of vision.

"I'm assuming you'll report this to Adam?"

"Yes, of course," Sadie said, gathering her jacket. "He'll want to know about this."

"Better you than me," Rosa said.

Sadie sighed. Goddess help anyone that dared to give a berserker bad news.

CHAPTER 3

*E*rich sat in his leather recliner, a bottle of bourbon in his hand. He hadn't bothered to turn on the lights. Coming down from an uncontrolled berserker rage always left him raw, weak, and overstimulated. Even the dimmest of light felt like sharp knives stabbing his brain. It's what they called going nuclear and felt absolutely amazing at the time. He didn't remember much, but the powerful, animalistic euphoria was etched into his mind.

He didn't feel so great at that moment, though. Taking a deep drink from the bottle, he relaxed into the chair. The cocktail of hormones and liquor was starting to calm him and he sighed as the familiar heaviness of his limbs threatened to overtake him. Maybe he should drink some coffee. His life was about to be turned upside down and he needed to be alert.

Erich's eyes flew open as someone banged on his door. When had he fallen asleep?

"Erich? We know you're in there. Open up," a deep voice said from the other side of the door. "Open it or we break it down."

He walked to the door and hesitated, his hand on the knob. He'd been free for seven years. If he opened the door, he'd be opening himself to the possibility of being sucked back into that life. A life of blood and violence. His mind flashed to the mess of bodies he had left in the alley. Apparently blood and violence was going to follow him no matter how far he ran.

"That's a good boy," a different voice said. "Open up."

Of course. Even without their rage, berserkers had advanced senses. They could hear everything on the other side of the door, even his breathing. Rolling his eyes, he turned the lock and cracked the door open. Accepting the invitation, the two men pushed the door open and walked in. One had the customary light hair and blue eyes common amongst Northmen, while the other had the brown skin and tightly curled hair of his mixed heritage.

"I'm not a fucking dog, Tyrell." Erich shuffled back to his chair.

The blond man grinned. "Aww...don't cry, princess."

Erich could only glare at him as he sank into his chair, not trusting his legs to support his weight.

Tyrell hooked his thumbs in his pockets and looked around. "This is where you've been staying this whole time? What a shit hole."

Erich ignored him. He had deliberately chosen this apartment to keep him grounded. He didn't need fancy cars and expensive toys. Give him four walls and a good book and he was a happy man. He didn't expect someone like Ty to understand. The guy went through gadgets like toilet paper.

"That's enough, Ty. Go check the rest of the apartment." Wade Ahmadi Fredrikson was the organization's second in command and had been Erich's best friend before he had left. Despite being a natural peacekeeper, he didn't allow any bullshit under his watch.

Erich picked up his bottle. He was not in the mood for Ty's bullshit right now. Wade stepped into his field of vision.

"How you doing, Erich?" His brown eyes were soft with concern as he took in Erich's wounds.

"I've been better."

"Can you move?"

Erich nodded. "Barely. I'm about to crash big time."

Wade slapped him on the shoulder and stood. "Okay, we'll make it quick." He stared down at him. "You have to come back to headquarters. You know that, right?" Erich nodded and watched as his former best friend rummaged through his apartment, looking for any intel that might endanger their mission.

"You won't find anything," he said. "I purged that life a long time ago."

"Fair enough," Wade said, closing the drawer he had been looking through. Wade picked up the photo of Erich and Nia taken at the grand opening of his fighting gym. "Is this your girl?"

"No, she's a friend. She's staying with me for a while. Works for me at the gym."

Wade raised an eyebrow. "But she's just a friend?"

"Yes," Erich said through gritted teeth. "Don't even think about it, asshole."

Wade held the frame for a beat before putting it down and holding his hands up as if in surrender. "The thought's already gone," he said with a grin.

"Yeah, right," Erich said, though to be fair, if he wanted to set Nia up with any of his friends, Wade would be his first choice. The man was a solid fighter and loyal to a fault. But he was also a berserker. Erich wouldn't wish that on any woman.

Tyrell came from the back hallway carrying Erich's black duffle bag. "Apartment's clear, but the bathroom's a mess."

Wade pulled out his phone. "I'm on it."

Ty fixed Erich with an intense stare. "When is your room-mate coming home?"

"Nia is working until the gym closes," he said. "She'll be back around eleven."

"Put a rush on it," Wade said into his phone before slapping it shut. "Let's go, brother."

With Wade's help, Erich stood to his feet, his body feeling like lead and his knee screaming in protest. The men painstakingly made their way out of his apartment building toward the black SUV that was illegally parked in a no-parking zone. Even though he had asked for their help, he briefly considered making a run for it, but in his state, he wouldn't make it two steps. Besides, there's no way he'd escape one of the many throwing knives that Wade kept hidden in pockets and sleeves. While Wade wouldn't aim to kill, he would put a knife in a strategic place with surprising accuracy.

Erich collapsed in the back seat. As Tyrell pulled away from the curb, a white van pulled into the parking lot. Despite the silhouette of a woman pushing a vacuum cleaner on the side, Erich knew it was the organization's cleaning crew arriving to rid his apartment of any evidence. Erich leaned his head against the headrest and closed his eyes.

"Eyes open," Ty ordered, watching him in the rearview mirror. "Don't you dare crash on me. I'm not carrying your ass into the building."

Erich forced his eyes open and glared at him. Of all the people he was about to let back in to his life, Tyrell Hannsen was the worst. The only thing going for him was his superiority in hand to hand combat, a useful skill since his smart ass mouth tended to get him into trouble. Erich's teeth made a clicking sound as he ground them together. He didn't know how, but he was going to find a way to kick his ass. While Ty had skill, Erich had superior speed. *He'll figure something out.* He grinned in anticipation.

Wade checked his watch. "ETA is fifteen minutes."

They rode for a while in silence. Erich stared out of the window at the passing landscape. His apartment was strategically located on the invisible barrier between the city and the suburbs, and soon the tall buildings quickly gave way to sprawling neighborhoods and eventually scattered industrial parks.

As Tyrell turned the SUV down a winding lane, Erich caught a glimpse of the headquarters building. From the outside, it looked like any other office building, a monument of glass and concrete. It was the kind of building that any normal passerby wouldn't give a second thought. What the humans did not know, however, was that the building stood between the Seedy underbelly of the paranormal world and their soft, carefree lives.

The nondescript SUV drove past the front parking lot that was used by the civilian employees who helped keep the public face of the business running, and headed around to the back of the building. They drove straight into the private parking garage that was coded for clan use only.

"Let's go, Sleeping Beauty," Tyrell said, grabbing Erich's duffel bag from the back seat. Erich stood and looked around the familiar parking garage. *Odinshield Protection Agency.* To the civilian world, it looked like a normal, mildly successful company that focused on protecting rich assholes and heads of state. The classified version was that government agencies turned to Odinshield to achieve some of the riskier missions that the protective force and intelligence agencies couldn't legally do.

The even more classified version was a mission that very few humans were aware of. Humanity went about their lives secure in the knowledge that they were the controlling occupants of this planet. Things like demons, witches, and were-wolves were something out of fantasy stories.

Odinshield knew better.

After punching in a code, the three men entered the underground entrance and stopped in front of the elevator. During the day, the first floor was bustling with humans doing the work needed to keep this place running. As a result, they sometimes needed a more secretive way to get in that was outside of human eyes.

Berserker work could get messy.

The ride up was silent, with Erich sandwiched between Wade and Tyrell like they thought he was going to burst out of the elevator and make a run for it.

Wade checked his phone. "The boss is out until tomorrow, so we'll take you to a room."

Erich nodded. It was probably for the best. He didn't think he could handle any more obstacles that stood between him and a bed. His nerves were fried, and he was about to crash hard. Tyrell was already walking a fine line between getting his head ripped off and getting to live out the rest of his life in relative peace.

They briefly walked down a hall and stopped in front of a door. "This is you," Wade said, holding his watch in front of the electronic sensor. The panel beeped and Wade typed in a four-digit code. Erich recognized it as their unit number from back in their time in the protective force. The panel beeped again.

"That's your key to the door," Wade said as he pushed his way into the room. Erich's eyes focused onto the bed and his legs made their way over to it as if of their own volition.

"Wait, before you crash—"

"Too late," Ty said.

Erich fell onto the bed and it was lights out.

❄

He woke for the second time, disoriented and confused. As the room came into focus, memories from the previous night flooded into his mind. Dark alley. Berserker rage. Wade and Ty picking him up.

Oh yeah.

Erich sat up, grimacing at the sharp pain in his side. Lifting his shirt, he stared at the long cut that went from his abs to his back. The bleeding had stopped, healing much faster than a human would, but the wound still looked raw and angry. He dropped his shirt and scrubbed his face with his hand.

"Good, you're up," Tyrell said as he came through the door to the adjoining room. Erich cursed. Of all the people to see first thing in the morning, why did it have to be the most annoying, sarcastic asshole here?

Tyrell tossed a clean shirt into his lap. It was black of course. They all wore black. It hid the sight of blood. "Get dressed. The boss is waiting."

The elevator ride to the top floor was thankfully silent. Tyrell seemed to be lost in his own thoughts, and Erich was happy to let him have his privacy. The doors opened directly into the penthouse suite and Erich followed Tyrell through an opulent sitting area, past an empty reception desk, and toward a set of heavy, oak double doors. After a sharp rap with his knuckles, Tyrell let himself in and motioned for Erich to walk ahead of him.

Adam Birkeland, leader of the Triton City Ulfhednar clan, rested against his desk, one hip perched on the side to support his weight. He acknowledged Tyrell with a nod before turning back to his phone call.

Erich sat in one of the plush chairs. Odinshield had done well for itself in his absence. With generous Seed money from Wolveshire, Odinshield had always had money, but now everything had been upgraded.

"You must have some lucrative contracts," he said.

Tyrell's face went blank. "We do okay."

Erich rolled his eyes. He had forgotten how secretive the business could be. Although it was necessary, the lack of trust stung a little. He had left the organization to live a peaceful civilian life. It's not like he had turned traitor and started hanging with the Frelshednar or anything.

Suppressing a sigh, he turned his attention to the man on the phone. His sheer size seemed to take over the room, and Erich had the familiar desire to snap to attention out of respect. He resisted, though, choosing instead to slump even further.

Adam finished his call and set the phone on his desk. Crossing his arms, he glared at Erich with sharp blue eyes.

"Leave us," Adam ordered. Without a word, Tyrell jumped up and hurried out of the room. Erich stood and faced his former chieftain.

"Hello, brother."

CHAPTER 4

All hail the Seed.

Sadie woke with a gasp, the familiar words echoing in her ears. Her fingers instinctively went to the small raised scar on her inner arm. She drew a deep breath as the familiar surroundings pierced her sleep-fogged mind. Inhale for three seconds, hold your breath, exhale for three seconds. Repeat.

It had become a morning ritual.

She was in her bedroom. Sparsely decorated, but functional and comfortable. Her sister hummed along with the radio somewhere in the apartment. The clock on her nightstand read three in the afternoon.

She rubbed her hand over her face and sighed. She'd thought she was over those nightmares, but after years of restful sleep, they had suddenly started happening again.

Her mind flashed to the young alara who was lying dead on a cold metal table in the morgue. How many people had he healed? How many lives had he saved with his healing power, only to end up murdered with his throat ripped out.

The world was an unfair place.

All hail the Seed.

Sadie jumped out of bed as if movement would erase the memory of her past. The Children of Light. Her family. Had they traveled to Triton City? Were they the ones killing alara? As a child, she had participated in hundreds of blood rituals, but they were all relatively safe, as far as blood sacrifices go. After the tragic death of her older brother, the Children had always been careful not to take too much. They had lost one alara, they didn't want to lose another. She fingered the raised scar on her inner arm.

The alarm on her phone sounded. She sighed. At least her nightmare had been close to her normal wake up time. Odinshield. Dead alara. Sadie grimaced. She was not looking forward to telling her boss about her new discovery.

When she was first approached about working for Odinshield Protection Agency, she was hesitant. She had loved working at the small free clinic downtown, but the meager pay made it hard to pay the bills, let alone her student loans. Odinshield offered an insanely generous salary, with the only caveat being that she not reveal the true purpose of the organization.

Even with the big salary, she had chosen to remain in the small two-bedroom apartment that she shared with her younger sister, Lauren. They were both barely home anyway, so it was best to save the money for when her too-good-to-be-true job was taken away for some reason. Even with her recent good fortune, she was always worried that the rug would get pulled from under her feet, a byproduct of her childhood, no doubt.

Shaking herself from her thoughts, because there was no way she was going to go down that rabbit hole, Sadie put on her slippers and padded out of her bedroom. Lauren was sitting at the dining room table, sipping on her coffee and looking at her cell phone.

"Put that thing away," Sadie said as she made her way into the kitchen to grab a cup of coffee. She drowned it with french vanilla creamer, stirring until the coffee was light tan. "It's too early to check social media."

Lauren rolled her eyes. "I wish I was checking social media. No, I'm looking at my assignments for the week."

Cradling her mug, Sadie collapsed on the plushy couch closest to the dining area, stabilizing her body with her hand as she sunk deep into the cushion. She hated the thing. It was impractically soft and the pale yellow color reminded her of pus. It looked like a boil right after it had been lanced, but Lauren loved it. She said it was like a soft teddy bear giving her a hug. Thus, the Great Big Boil remained in a place of honor in the living room. Sadie gestured toward the stack of books in the middle of the table. "Are all of those for this semester?"

Lauren nodded and brushed rogue strands of her hair away from her pale face. Too pale actually. They both had their mother's brown hair and brown eyes but that was where the similarities ended. While Lauren was short, like their mother and her father, Sadie inherited her height from her father, who stood well over six feet.

The Children of Light were not big on monogamy.

"Yes. I'm taking a full load this semester and each class has, like three books." She stared at the pile solemnly. "I don't know if I'm going to be able to keep working at the Cookie Hut. These classes sound crazy."

Sadie heaved herself off of the Great Big Boil and set her coffee on the dining room table. She picked up the top book and casually flipped through it.

"I agree," Sadie said. "The last thing you need is to be too stressed to finish school."

Lauren looked relieved. "Good. I was afraid you'd want me to keep working."

"Why would you even worry about that?"

"Because I won't be able to help with the bills. Hell, I won't even be able to pay for gas or my cell phone plan." The worried look flashed across her face again.

This was why Sadie hated secrets. As part of her job agreement, she had vowed to not reveal the true mission of Odinshield Protection Agency, including the fact that their line of work was insanely lucrative. Because of that agreement, she had let Lauren keep her job under the pretense that she needed help with the bills. With Triton City having such a high cost of living, it wasn't so hard to believe. As far as Lauren was concerned, Sadie worked for a small protection agency that no one had heard of and made slightly more than she had earned in her clinic downtown.

Setting the book down, Sadie enveloped her sister in a hug. "Don't worry about the bills," she said. "I make enough to cover everything, including your phone and gas."

"Really? Did you get a raise or something?"

Sadie straightened and walked into the kitchen. She turned on the faucet and pretended to rinse the sink. She had been working on which story to tell her sister, and hadn't really decided on the right one. By story, she meant lie, of course. Something she'd been doing a lot lately.

"Odinshield has taken on a new long term contract. I got a raise," she said.

Lauren jumped up and clapped her hands. "Congratulations! That's amazing!"

Sadie smiled. "So you see? We don't have to worry anymore."

Lauren bounced over to her and gave her a hug. "This is such good news. You definitely deserve this. You work way too much.

Sadie pasted a smile on her face as her heart sank. Lies always birthed new lies. Her new job had been both a blessing and a curse. At least she wouldn't have to lie to her sister anymore. She watched as Lauren chattered happily and gathered her school books. Sadie's phone chirped in her back pocket.

Something went down last night. Will need you in a few.

Sadie sighed. Odinshield's missions have been getting more frequent and dangerous. It's come to the point where the guys hardly have time to heal up before heading out into the field again. Berserkers have accelerated healing but even they need a day or two to recover.

"Trouble?" Lauren asked.

Sadie rolled her eyes. "Of course. Being careful is not in those guys' vocabulary," she said, heading to her room to get dressed. "Dinner tonight?"

Lauren shook her head. "I'm hanging out with Zane."

Of course, ever since they had met on campus, she had been spending almost every evening with her new boyfriend. While Sadie was happy that her sister was happy, she wished they spent more time together. Between both of their schedules, they only had these small bits of time to catch up.

Her phone chirped again. Duty called and as Odinshield's only medical support, she couldn't afford to be late.

CHAPTER 5

*A*dam looked pissed. Erich sighed and subconsciously stretched his shoulders as if preparing for a fight. They had been close their whole lives, Erich had followed in his brother's footsteps well into adulthood. They had both played sports and excelled on and off the field. After Adam had joined the protective force, Erich had signed up as soon as he was of age.

"Tell me what happened," Adam said, the softness of his voice at odds with the hardness of his eyes.

Erich sighed and ran his hand through his short hair. "Not much to say. I was going about my life when the Frelshednar tried to kill me."

"You're sure it was the Frelshednar?"

"Yes," Erich said. "At least one of them were. He had the Sign of the Bear tattooed on his arm."

Adam was quiet for a moment, his gazed fixed on the floor as if he was deep in thought. "Tell me exactly what they said."

"To be honest, I don't remember. I was walking home when a couple of guys approached me. They wanted my wallet and when I didn't produce it, they threw a punch." Erich hesitated. "I don't remember anything after that, just waking up."

Erich grimaced as Adam's head snapped up. That was the part he was hoping to avoid. "You went nuclear?"

Erich didn't want to answer. He had trained for years under the rules of the Ulfhednar to control his rage and use the strength of the berserker without losing his mind. To give in and become a mindless animal was a sign of weakness. A sign that you didn't have control over your inner beast. Still, it had happened, and if he wanted Odinshield's help dealing with this, he was going to have to be honest.

"Yes," he said, looking Adam directly in the eye. Short and sweet. He wasn't going to make excuses or rationalizations. On the outside, he was a solid rock, but internally, his stomach clenched. Would he forever be the little boy seeking his big brother's approval?

The silence stretched between them. Adam stood with a sigh and moved to the back of his desk.

"It looks like your little experiment is over. I was hoping you would succeed. To live a normal life has been the dream of some of us for a long time." Adam's eyes shuttered as he stared at something in the middle distance.

The last thing Erich wanted to do was bring up Adam's past. It was a subject best left in the deep, dark corner of the mind.

"I had to at least try to. I'm not like you. I can't just accept that this is who I am. I'm not some crazy beast."

"There are about five bodies in an alley that say otherwise."

Erich sat back, his eyes locked on a random spot on the expensive Turkish rug. He was a grown man. Sulking was beneath him, but whenever he was around his older brother he tended to fall into old habits. "They weren't all dead."

Adam scrubbed his hand over his face and sighed. "Another complication that we're going to have to clean up."

Erich frowned. "You sound like I asked for this," he said. "Those assholes jumped me. As far as I'm concerned, they deserved what they got.

"The issue isn't that you defended yourself," Adam said. "It's that you went nuclear."

Erich held his tongue. Anything he said at that point would just make things worse. Besides, as much as he hated to admit it, Adam was right.

"What's done is done," Adam said. "You belong here. With your brothers who can help you get this under control. We are not meant to go about things alone."

"I wasn't alone. I had Nia," Erich said.

"I'm aware of her," Adam said. Erich must have looked shocked because he smirked. "You may have left, but I still consider you one of us. What I don't know is the extent of your relationship with her. She lives with you, correct?"

"Yes, she fell on hard times, so I let her stay with me until she got back on her feet."

Adam raised an eyebrow. "For four years? Is she your girl?"

Erich crossed his arms. "She's a friend."

"Does she know about us?"

"No, she thinks supes are fairy tale characters."

Adam nodded. "Good. Then ditching her won't be a problem."

Erich straightened. "I don't know what you think is going on here, but I will not be ditching her. Nia is like a sister to me."

"She's not like us," Adam said. "Listen, I used to think we had a shot at a normal life, and believe me, I tried to figure out a way to make it happen. Hell, I lived it when I was using the serum, but I was half a man. This animal inside of us is larger than lattes and bullshit walks in the park. We made an oath to protect Triton City, and we were put on this world for that purpose."

Erich stared at the floor. Only in his brother's presence would he allow such a sign of weakness. Adam was right. During the years in the protective force, when Adam and Wade had been a part of Project Red Oak and had controlled their rage with the Verilium serum, life had felt empty. The serum had allowed them to bend their rage to their will, but it had also dampened all other emotions. Partying, good food, even sex had lost all joy. Without even the thrill of battle to bring them any happiness, suicide had definitely been on the table.

"I really thought I could do it," he whispered. Seven years. Seven years of keeping his beast under control only to have it wiped away by one bad night.

"I know brother. Out of all of us, I figured you'd be the one to make it on the outside."

Erich closed his eyes and sighed. "So what has happened in my absence? I see that Wade is still your number 2 and Tyrell is even more of a smart ass."

"As you can see, we've had a few upgrades since you've been gone," Adam said.

"I noticed."

"A couple of new guys have joined us. We make six now, counting you."

The silence stretched between them. Erich scanned the plush decor of Adam's office. Life had moved on in his absence and apparently business was good. Not that he was bitter about that. People moved on, especially older brothers. His life had been pretty nice as well. He had had an easy job, a pretty girl now and then, and a couple of friends to pass the time with. Now it was gone.

"So what happens now? I won't let the Frelshednar get

away with this," he said.

Adam pushed away from the desk. "We're going to report this to Wolveshire."

"Seriously? What the hell are those old fuckers going to do?"

Adam gave him a withering look. "We do this by the book, brother. We are not going to go vigilante and start raising hell, understand?"

Erich frowned but held his tongue. He couldn't say he was surprised by Adam's reaction, or inaction. Adam had always followed the strict code of Ulfhednar to a T. Even a murder attempt on his brother's life wouldn't be enough for him to break the rules.

"Come on," Adam said. "Let's have the doctor take a look at that cut."

Erich stood. "You have a doctor, now?" He asked as they headed toward the elevator.

"Yep. Sadie Carmichael."

"A woman?"

Adam stopped and faced him. "Yes and she's off limits. You understand?"

Erich nodded. The last thing on his mind was the fairer sex. "Got it, boss. No touching the doc."

The elevator ride was quiet as each brother was lost in his own thoughts. The knot in Erich's stomach had lessened during his conversation with Adam. It was almost like some inner part of himself was relieved to be back under the control of the Ulfhednar.

Being on his own had been great. The freedom to do whatever he had wanted with whoever he wanted was nice. But he had to always be on alert so that no one knew what he really was. People tended to get a little uncomfortable when a supernatural killing machine was in their midst.

The doors dinged open and Erich followed his brother

through a series of secure doors, pressing his watch against each keypad to gain entrance. They walked through what looked like the last set of security doors, down a long hallway and into a large medical room. There were four curtained off areas, each with a bed surrounded by medical equipment.

"What…Why do you have a whole clinic?"

"Things have gotten a little hot since you left. We've had to make a few changes."

"No shit," Erich muttered. He froze as a woman entered from the back office bringing with her the most tantalizing scent of lavender and vanilla.

"Dr. Carmichael, this is my brother Erich." The woman looked up from the electronic tablet she was holding and smiled. He'd had his share of beautiful women, but he had never seen anyone as captivating as the woman in front of him.

She had the type of coloring that made it hard to guess her ancestry. Her rich brown eyes were framed by thin-rimmed glasses and a lock of honey brown hair dangled in front of her face. Erich's brain felt electrified as he focused on her lips. Beautiful, luscious, and very kissable. As she smiled up at him, his shoulders relaxed, like he had found his place in the world and could finally die a happy man. For the first time in his life, the rage that was always simmering just below his skin was calm.

He inhaled. The scent of her made his head swim. All of his senses were both calm and heightened at the same time, and he wanted nothing more than to bury his face into her neck and breath and taste her.

She gasped as he pulled her body against his, her soft curves molding and yielding against the strength of his body. The sound of her gasp was music to his ears. Her scent took over his senses. He said some words. Mindless ramblings. She placed her hand against his chest and pushed against it.

Against him.

Against him? Erich froze. He felt strong hands on his shoulder, pulling him away from his woman. He ignored them, focusing on the small hand against his chest. She pushed against him again. Her eyes looked wide and confused.

"Erich, let go of the doc. Let her go!" His brother's voice sounded angry. Authoritative. Erich blinked as his foggy mind began to clear.

Sadie was still pressed against him. Her face was flushed and her soft brown eyes filled with confusion. Erich quickly released her, mumbling an apology.

She was silent, just watching as Adam pulled him out of the room and into the hallway. He couldn't take his eyes off of her but held back the urge to push his brother to the side and finish what he had started.

Had there been fear in her eyes?

Adam pushed him against the wall and held him in place with his arm.

"Cool it, brother," Adam growled. Erich froze as the order from his chieftain pierced his foggy brain. He glanced at the door but the doctor had closed it. "Breathe."

Erich pushed him away and stalked down the hallway. The last thing he remembered was seeing the new doc and thinking about how beautiful she was. He had definitely felt a connection between them, on his end, at least.

"Who is she?" he demanded.

Adam watched him, his eyes wary. "Sadie. She's the unit's doctor," he said, slowly as if talking to someone insane.

Erich stared at the closed door, ignoring the desire to kick it down and claim his woman right on her desk. His woman. What in the hell was wrong with him? Adam stepped into his field of vision.

"You good?"

Erich nodded.

"I need you to say it, brother."

Erich took a deep breath and let it out. "I'm good."

"Want to tell me why you decided to manhandle my doctor? A civilian under my direct protection?" Erich straightened. Now that he was back, Sadie was under Erich's protection, not his brothers. As far as he was concerned, fulfilling her needs was his job. If she was hungry, he would bring her food. If she was fearful, he would protect her, and pity anyone who would get in his way.

Erich groaned and scrubbed his face with his hand. What was he thinking? He didn't even know this woman, and yet he was willing to burn the world down to make her happy.

"I don't know what happened back there. I just…wasn't myself."

Adam studied him, his face worried. The secure door swished open and Tyrell and another man sprinted through. "Yo! We got Sadie's alarm. What's going on?" Tyrell said.

The other man jogged down the hall and rapped on the doctor's door. "Sadie, you okay?"

Erich's stomach clenched at the sound of the feminine voice as she answered. Adam punched him in the shoulder. "Cool it!" He ordered. Erich took a step back and raised his hands.

"I didn't do anything," he protested.

Tyrell eyed him, his face serious for once. "Dude, your eyes shifted gold," He said, referring to the telltale sign that a berserker was about to lose his shit. Ty turned to Adam. "What is this?"

Adam looked grim. "I don't know, but Erich needs to get his shit together." He punched his brother's shoulder again for emphasis.

Erich took another breath and let it out slowly. As much as he hated to admit it, seeing the doctor had affected him in a way he's never felt before. He'd seen plenty of hot women, but there was something about her that made him want to protect her and kill any man who dared breath her air.

"I'm fine. I can control myself."

"There's no way you're seeing the doc." Erich had forgotten about the other man who had come running in with Tyrell. It was hard to forget him now as he stood glaring at him, his light grey eyes icy and arms crossed. Erich straightened his shoulders.

"And who's going to stop me?" He challenged, stepping up to him. Unsurprisingly, the man held his ground, a living barrier between Erich and his women. His woman. Damn, he did it again.

"It's fine, Brandt. I'll see him." All four men stiffened at the sound of the feminine voice. Erich's breath caught as he looked around the new guy to catch a glimpse of her. Despite her slim stature, she seemed to fill the entire doorway.

The man named Brandt walked toward her. Too close, in Erich's opinion. This time, he sensed his body reacting and took a deep breath to suppress the urge to rip the guy's head off.

"No," Brandt said. "This guy is obviously not in control. We don't know what he'll do."

Sadie fixed Erich with a stare, her eyes shooting lasers into his skull. "Will you hurt me?" She asked.

"Never," he blurted. He wasn't even aware he was speaking before the word was already out of his mouth. Sadie nodded.

"Good," she said. She nodded at Adam. "Bring him in. I'll see him." Without waiting for a response, she turned and walked into the room.

CHAPTER 6

*W*hile the men stood in the hallway threatening her patient with increasingly creative methods of punishment, Sadie returned her stun gun to the holster at her waist. There wasn't much that could stop a berserker once he was deep into his rage, but 50,000 volts of electricity was enough to slow him down. For a little while, at least.

She had never claimed that her job was without risk.

Having it around made her feel better. Gave her some control. She couldn't sit back like a sheltered kitten while the men made decisions for her. She had spent years under the thumb of other people, doing as she had been told, and she wasn't ever going back to that.

Still, when Adam had pushed Erich into the hall, she had followed protocol and pressed her panic button. She was a doctor, and despite any warm fuzzies she was feeling, logic would always win. Hopefully.

The voices in the hall grew heated. Sadie sighed and picked up her tablet. It sounded like the guys were going to take a while, so she might as well research her patient's medical history.

Erich's irises had flashed gold the instant he had laid eyes on her, a sign that the berserker rage was about to take over. As a berserker, he could have ripped her to shreds without breaking a sweat, and would have probably enjoyed it. But deep down, she knew he wouldn't have hurt her. Call it a sixth sense, or woman's intuition, but she'd always been an excellent judge of character. Besides, his history with the Ulfhednar was a good indication that he had his rage under control.

The men at Odinshield were different than other berserkers. They followed the strict meditation regimen that was mandated by the Head Council and trained day in and day out to control their bodies and emotions. Most of them had the ability to reap the benefits of their berserker rage - increased strength and speed, imperviousness to pain, and elevated levels of wild aggression - all without the downfall of being mindless and out of control. With the proper training, it was the best of both worlds. But despite their efforts, they still had the potential to go nuclear, and that usually left a path of death and destruction.

Berserkers coming down from an episode tended to spend the next couple of days in a subdued state as their bodies adjusted to not being killing machines. But not this one. It was as if he hadn't gone nuclear at all. His presence had filled the room like he owned the place and the look in his eyes told her that his ownership extended to her.

Strangely enough, she wasn't scared. With other berserker, a sign of losing control would have filled her with panic, but she had only felt curious about his odd reaction. Her cheeks heated at the memory of her body pressed against his. His face serious. His eyes glowing gold as he looked down at her. Despite the gentleness of his touch, his body was pure hardness and muscle. No, she wasn't afraid he would hurt her. She was afraid, because for those few seconds, she didn't trust herself to remain in control. Deep down, she suspected that all of the walls and barriers she had erected against the outside world would crumble under his golden gaze.

A search for Erich's medical record turned up empty. Sadie frowned. He looked too old to be a new recruit, most berserkers have their first episode in their teenage years, so he must have history with the organization. Wouldn't Adam's brother be in Odinshield's records?

While the men in the hallway continued to argue, she exited out of the medical application and opened Wolveshire's historical files. Adam had mentioned his brother while discussing his time in the protective force. Maybe there was more information in the files he had stolen from the lab.

Sadie smiled as her search resulted in a single file. Tapping on the icon, she quickly skimmed through the information. Like all Ulfhednar, Erich had trained at Wolveshire during his teenage years. When he came of age, he had followed in his older brother's footsteps and enlisted in the Sardovian protective force. Judging by his onboarding dates, he had quickly been recruited into Project Red Oak, a mission that had sought to control the berserker rage by manipulating the men on a hormonal level.

A sharp knock on the doorjamb drew her attention away from her research. Adam led his brother to one of the examination beds. Tyrell and Brandt were right on his heels. They were following so close to him, they could have shared body heat.

She motioned for him to hop onto the examination table. Erich hesitated before walking stiffly to the table. He was so tall that no hop was needed and he just sat down and looked at her expectantly. His guards crowded around him, ready to intervene if he made a wrong move.

Sadie stepped closer and opened her senses. Rapid heartbeat. Elevated blood pressure. Pain. He had visible wounds on his face and arms, but none seemed bad enough to cause the level of pain he was feeling.

"Are you injured?" she asked.

Erich shrugged. "Not really. I have a cut on my side and I tweaked my knee."

"Take off your shirt," she ordered. Erich instantly obeyed. His eyes burned into hers, intense and fierce. Sadie swallowed hard. She didn't know why, but she was pretty sure that if she had told him to jump off of a bridge, he would have complied with a smile. She forced herself to look away and turn her attention to her patient's cut.

It stretched from his abdomen to his back and extended to his right arm, just below the Ulfhednar wolf tattoo that all of the men at Odinshield had somewhere on their bodies. His cut was still seeping, and the wound looked angry. She reached out and hovered her hand over the wound, closing the rest of her senses so that only she and the body underneath her hand existed. From the state of his wound, a blade was used in a slashing and twisting motion. The wound was free of debris, but infection was brewing. She neutralized the foreign bacteria. She could have completely healed his wound, but in her experience, otherwise healthy patients were better off if the body naturally healed itself. Besides, berserkers tended to heal quickly. No point in tiring herself out.

Drawing a shuddering breath, Sadie glanced at her patient. His blue eyes were intense as he stared into the distance. His face was a mask of stone, refusing to show even a shred of emotion. As if he could sense her interest, his eyes flicked to hers. A streak of electricity shot between them before she abruptly looked away. He apparently felt the same if his sudden change of heart rate was any indication.

"It's not deep and will heal in time." She crossed the room and grabbed some supplies. "I'll have to sew it up. Keep it dry and try to take it easy."

Erich grunted as she poured antiseptic over the cut. Tyrell chuckled. "Wuss."

Erich's head snapped up. He gently pushed Sadie's hands away from his wound as his body tensed, ready to spring into action.

"Everyone cool it," Adam ordered. "Ty, out. We can take it from here." With a smirk and a mock salute, Tyrell left the room.

Sadie watched her patient's face as he followed Ty's exit with his eyes. Both rage and shame simmered within his eyes. As Ty disappeared through the threshold, Erich slowly relaxed and turned his attention back to her.

Sadie smiled. "Are we ready?" Erich gave a stiff nod, and she went back to work on his cut.

"I'm sorry," he said to no one in particular. "I'm just... tired."

"It's okay," Sadie said. "You've had a rough night."

"It's not just that," Erich said. "The way I reacted when I first saw you..." Erich shook his head. "That was weird. I'm not that guy. I promise you."

Sadie didn't know what to say, but he seemed to be expecting some sort of answer. She was frozen under the weight of his gaze. This must have been what deer felt when they encountered headlights bearing down upon them, only instead of a car, she had the full intensity of an emotional berserker focused on her.

Adam slapped him on the shoulder, breaking their connection. "No worries, brother. We'll get you sorted."

Ignoring the slight tremor in her hands, she finished

closing his wound and covered it with sterile gauze. She stared at her handiwork, afraid to meet his eyes for fear of what she would feel. By the time she gained the nerve to look up, he was already reaching for his shirt.

"You're all set," she said. "Come back tomorrow so I can take a look at it." Erich nodded mutely, his face unreadable.

"Has the shipment arrived?"

Sadie blinked, momentarily confused at the sudden change of subject. She wasn't surprised, though. Adam tended to be direct and to the point. Before she could answer, Brandt cut in.

"Do you want me to take Erich out of here?" He shot a glare at her patient.

Adam shook his head. "Let him stay. Now that he's back, he needs to get caught up."

That seemed to get Erich's attention. "What's going on?"

Brandt shook his head. "You sure? He's been out for years. Who knows what he's been doing all that time. He could have fallen in with Haralson's clan for all we know."

Erich drew in a sharp breath and stood. "Back off, asshole. I may have left, but I'm still a brother. I bear the wolf mark just like everyone else here." Brandt ignored him, his eyes trained on his chieftain.

"Erich is my brother, by blood and by clan. I trust him with my life. You may never trust him, but I ask that you do trust my judgment on this."

Brandt remained silent, arms folded and his pale grey eyes cold as ice. Sadie gave him a sympathetic look. With his history, trust was hard to come by. Still, her boss had asked her a question and, unlike Brandt, she had no reason to be distrustful.

"Not yet. I spoke with the supplier yesterday. Shipping is delayed. They didn't have the proper documents to travel through Mti."

"How hard is it to get travel letters?"

"Very hard, apparently," Sadie said with a shrug. "He said the shipment will be delayed at least a month."

If it were any other berserker, Sadie would feel a little hesitant about being the bearer of bad news. Most untrained berserkers would absolutely kill the messenger. But Adam was the paragon of self-control. She was beginning to wonder if he possessed the berserker gene at all.

Still, there was always the chance that this one bit of bad news or one small insult would be the catalyst for a full-blown melt down. It was bound to happen eventually and Sadie did not want to be there when it did.

"Have you had a chance to stop by the morgue?" he asked, unflappable as always.

"I did, before I came here. The body was just like the others, drained of blood with lacerations on the neck."

Adam cursed. "Who was the victim?"

Sadie hesitated. Although she didn't fear Adam, he tended to be over protective. "It was an alara."

"That's the second one this month," Adam said.

"I know."

"You're moving into the compound," he ordered. Sadie knew this was coming, but she couldn't just uproot her life just because some jerk was on a killing spree.

"I don't think that's necessary—"

"Brandt, get Wade and Tyrell. Escort Sadie to her place so that she can pack."

Brandt nodded. "I'll bring the truck around front, doc," he said before leaving.

Sadie made another plea for normalcy. "Adam, I really don't think we have to do all of this. People get killed every day. This could just be a coincidence."

Adam ignored her. "Your sister should probably come

too. She may not be alara, but if they look for you at home, she may become collateral damage."

"Adam—"

"Enough, Sadie!" Adam ordered. "Some asshole is killing alara and draining them of their blood. You are under my protection. My job is to protect those under my protection."

"You are alara?"

Thankful for the distraction, Sadie smiled at her patient. "Yes."

Erich nodded. "It makes sense that you're a doctor."

"Most alara go into the medical field," Sadie said, eager to change the subject. "Every alara in my bloodline has been a healer. In fact, my distant grandmother was the personal healer for the royal family of Tutencourt." Sadie smiled. There had been quite a few alara in her family history but Healer Rose was by far the most celebrated. In the times of plagues and war, when there was the lack of basic modern medicine, being an alara was an honor. Her mind flicked to the young man laying pale and cold on the morgue table. They've gone from being honored by the wealthiest of nobles to being hunted and drained like animals.

Erich watched her, a slight smile on his lips. "You come from a noble bloodline."

Sadie scoffed. "That's where the honor ended, I'm afraid. My parents are...not as noble."

"Let me guess. They were really strict and expected you to be the best in everything," he said.

"Something like that." What else could she say? The last thing she wanted to talk about was blood rituals and purity ceremonies.

Her watched beeped.

Trucks out front. We're ready when you are.

"Is that Brandt with the truck?" Adam asked, slapping Erich on the shoulder to make him get up.

"Yep." Sadie sighed and turned to gather her bag. Now that Adam had gotten all alpha protective, it would be impossible to change his mind.

"Go ahead and get started. I have some business to finish but will meet you there later," he said.

"I don't want to put you out, Adam. I know you are busy. Between me, Ty, and Brandt, we should be fine."

Erich shrugged his shirt on over his shoulders. "No, it's not a problem. We'll be there."

Adam nodded. "You heard the man. We'll be there."

Sadie suppressed a smile as Erich's shot an apologetic look at his brother. Although Adam was the chieftain, brotherly bonds were hard to break.

"Okay, I guess I'll see you later." Sadie gave a little wave as she walked into the hall. Digging through her bag for her phone, she absentmindedly held her watch against each security pad as she walked down the hall. It was probably best to give her sister a heads up before she opened the door to find three huge warriors wanting to come in.

CHAPTER 7

*T*he two men walked down the hall in long efficient strides. At first glance, it was obvious that they were brothers, but upon closer examination the astute observer would notice that the younger stood slightly taller and leaner than the elder. Regardless, they both had the bearing of a warrior and radiated the aura of deadly efficiency.

"So, you snagged an alara," Erich said, the sound of his steel-toed boots echoed through the hall.

"Yeah, I didn't know she was special when I hired her, though. Our missions had been getting hairier, and we needed someone full time."

"Looks like you got lucky," Erich said.

"Yep, and I'd like to keep her in one piece." Adam stopped and poked a finger in Erich's chest. "That little stunt you pulled in front of the doc was bad form, brother."

Erich sighed and ran his hand through his short hair. "I know," he said. "It wasn't a stunt, though."

"Then what was it?"

Erich hesitated. "It was…something clicked in my head

and... I don't know why I hugged her like that. It was like I was on autopilot."

Adam's blue eyes narrowed into tiny slits. "The Ulfhednar do not tolerate rape. You know this."

Erich moved away. "Of course! I wasn't going to rape her. That didn't even cross my mind."

"Then what did cross your mind?" His voice hard.

"I don't know," Erich said. "I just felt totally at peace. With the way I was feeling, there's no way I could ever hurt her. Hell, if anyone hurts her, I will tear the motherfucker apart."

Adam watched him, his face unreadable. He seemed to come to a conclusion and sighed. "Speaking of tearing fuckers apart, let's go. We have video of your little party in the alley."

Erich followed his brother to a secure door, nondescript except for a black keypad to the right. Adam stopped before the door and turned to him.

"Stefen is our newest recruit. Super smart, but he can't control his rage. Not even a little," Adam said, keeping his voice low.

Erich frowned. "Really? How did he get through Tier three training?" Erich asked, referring to the extensive and sometimes painful training that berserkers who had problems controlling their rage had to go through. Recruits either successfully completed it, or were never heard from again. It was a guaranteed way to get a hundred percent success rate.

"No time," Adam said. "His situation is complicated. I just wanted to give you a heads up."

Adam waved his watch over the keypad and entered after hearing the solid click of the locking mechanism. Erich gaped as he stepped into the room. Before he had left, this area was a storage room, full of dusty boxes and metal filing cabinets left behind by the previous occupants. Now, the room was set up as a private command center. Monitors covered an entire back wall, while the right wall hummed with sleek technological equipment. To the left was a desk holding an expensive looking computer with two oversized monitors. The light-haired man at the desk didn't look up as they approached.

Adam rapped his knuckles on the desk. "Stefen."

The man jumped, his startled blue eyes flashing gold before returning to their normal color as they settled on Adam.

"Yes… Adam. I didn't hear you come in," he said.

"Good thing the door was locked," Erich muttered. Adam gave him a warning look.

"What are you working on?"

The man turned toward the screens. "I'm waiting on more footage on the latest alara attack. It happened in a parking garage, so there must have been cameras. I have a guy who can get into the shopping center's security feed."

"Santiago doesn't have it?"

Stefen shook his head. "No. It's not her case, so she can't get access. For some reason, the Feds have it under lock and key."

"Put that on hold for a second. I want to see the footage from last night."

For the first time, Stefen glanced at Erich. He gave a solemn nod before turning back to his keyboard. "If you give me a sec, I'll pull it up on the screens," he said, gesturing toward the wall of monitors. "Monitor seven. Video only, no sound."

Erich walked over to the screens and stood in front of the one marked seven. The screen flickered before showing a black and white video of an alley. He remembered the two men hanging out at the mouth of the alley, but there were apparently three others in the shadows behind them. The monitor flickered to a different viewpoint, and he saw himself walking toward the alley, his shoulders hunched against the wind.

As he reached the alley, the two men confronted him. The camera switched viewpoints again to show Erich having the conversation at the mouth of the alley. The three men in the shadows perked up and moved toward the entrance. Erich watched the screen as the conversation grew heated.

"They wanted my wallet," he said to no one in particular.

He didn't have to watch the video to know what happened next. One of the thugs grabbed his arm while the other cocked his arm back to punch him. Erich took a punch to his face, his head snapping back. That was where the clear memory of the event ended for him, but the video played on.

He righted himself and said something to the men. The men stepped back, startled. It was at that point where the men in the alley leaped forward and began raining punches and kicks on Erich. After a moment's hesitation, the original two men joined in.

Erich went down under the sea of bodies. One of the thugs lifted his head, his mouth wide open in a silent scream as he fell away, his leg bleeding and laying at an odd angle.

The pile of men shuddered before they all fell away in a tangle. Erich emerged from the pile, his arms raised and his mouth open. The veins in his neck stood out and his bright eyes sparkled as he yelled. The men scrambled to their feet but before they could launch their attack, Erich grabbed the closest one by the arm and slammed his fist into it, fracturing it in two. The man jerked in surprise just long enough for Erich to slam the sharp fractured bone into the man's own chest. He dropped like a stone.

Erich made quick work of the other two men, showing no mercy. Just after he delivered a fierce uppercut, he was grabbed from behind.

"That's the guy from the Frelshednar clan," Erich said.

Adam leaned in to get a closer look as the man swung his body and threw Erich against a dumpster. Erich was back on his feet in seconds, using his momentum to deliver a punch to the berserker's jaw. The berserker grinned as he wiped a string of blood from his mouth. The fight turned brutal, as each man worked to pummel the other to death. Where Erich's previous moves were strategic, he had now switched to something fierce and primal.

Watching the screen, Stefen cheered, his eyes glowing gold as he watched Erich body slam the other man and follow it up with savage kicks to his torso. The man rolled away and got to his feet. His mouth open in a silent snarl, he charged at Erich. Just before he made contact, Erich rolled to the side, grabbed the man by the back of the head, and slammed it into the wall. The berserker fell like a ton of bricks.

When no more thugs were standing, Erich lifted his head and howled. Movement caught his eye and Erich turned to find his first victim dragging his broken leg to the mouth of the alley. Erich grabbed the man on the sides of his head. The man slapped at his hands in a panic, but Erich's grip was strong. He held the thug in place, said something before leaning in and ripping the man's throat out with his teeth.

"That's my favorite move," Stefen said.

Erich sighed and rubbed his short hair. He had obviously known that the fight had turned deadly. The bloody bodies scattered around the alley didn't leave much to the imagination. But he had never seen himself go nuclear before. His chest swelled with pride at the same time as his stomach clenched in knots. He had left Odinshield to try to live a normal life and had succeeded for seven years. That one fight, that one moment of weakness, had burned everything to the ground. He turned away from the screens with a curse.

47

"Why would the Frelshednar try to kill me?" he asked. "Have things gotten worse since I've been gone?"

Stefen squinted at the monitor, deep in thought. "There's no proof that they are behind this," he said. "Yes, one of them was a berserker, but the others were supes. Maybe this was a rogue group. They could have picked you at random."

Adam studied the screen, his arms crossed. "That would be one hell of a coincidence," he said.

"No," Erich said, shaking his head. "That wasn't a normal mugging. They were trying to kill me."

"By using multiple species of men, they probably hoped to avoid detection. Hoped no one would be able to point it back to them," Stefen said.

"They thought they could take you down if there were a group of them," Adam said. "They thought wrong. You did the right thing, though you should have killed the Frelshednar bastard. One less psycho to deal with."

Erich shook his head. A berserker's ability to just shake off killing always shocked him. To most berserkers, taking a life was as natural as creating one, and almost as pleasurable. Erich was different. He'd never been comfortable killing and always avoided it. Well, except for when he went nuclear. Once the inner beast took over, all bets were off.

He absentmindedly ran his fingers over the wolf tattoo on his arm. They all had one. The mark to symbolize their clan. Organized centuries ago, the Ulfhednar clan believed in honor, duty, and protecting the weak. Its founder, Alarik VanHuburt, saw the potential that an organized and trained group of berserkers could bring to both the common man and royalty. It wasn't long before royal families from all over Tesselyn were willing to pay top dollar for the use of the berserker rage against their enemies.

One thing the Ulfhednar believed in, however, was control. Every member, whether born into the clan or recruited from the streets took a vow to never take an innocent life. Their training not only included lethal ways to kill, but also ways to remain in complete control. Through intense study, the best of them, like Adam, could maintain consciousness even while in their rage. Erich wasn't so lucky. Obviously.

Adam and Stefen had moved back to the computer monitor, obviously ready to move on to other things.

"Got it! My contact always comes through," Stefen said as he typed a series of keystrokes into the computer.

Adam leaned against the back of Stefen's chair, his eyes intent on the screen. His low curse was savage. He pulled out his phone. "It's me," he said. "Put 24/7 surveillance on Sadie right now. She goes nowhere without a brother with her."

Sadie's name sparked Erich's interest, and he made his way to Stefen's monitor. He could just make out the grainy images, but he couldn't deny what he was looking at. His hand reflexively went to his side where he normally kept his blade but came up empty. Right, civilians didn't carry knives. After looking at the carnage on the screen, he knew it was time to strap up. Whatever monster that could do that deserved to die, and if he so much as hurt a single hair on Sadie's head, it will die by his hand.

CHAPTER 8

*T*yrell collapsed on the couch and immediately flailed his arms as he sunk into the cushion. "Son of a...." he yelped. "What kind of crazy couch is this?"

Sadie hid her grin behind her hand, but she couldn't stop the giggle as she watched Tyrell try to roll off of the couch. "That's the Great Big Boil. Don't ask. Lauren loves it."

Tyrell frowned at it like he was debating whether to destroy the thing right then and there. Brandt clapped him on the back as he walked by and bent to lift one side. "Come on man, let's load it up."

Muttering under his breath, Tyrell grabbed the other side, and they carried the couch toward the door like it weighed nothing.

Lauren came into the living room, pulling her bright orange suitcase behind her. "Hey, be careful with that! It's precious."

"Sure, princess," Ty said, rolling his eyes.

Lauren turned to Sadie with wide eyes. "These are the guys you work for?"

"Yep," Sadie said. Her phone buzzed in her pocket and she reached for it.

Lauren waited for the brothers to take her couch out of the door before leaning in. "Oh my goddess! They are so hot! Especially the quiet one. His eyes are so unique."

Sadie laughed. "Calm down, sis. These guys are too old for you. Besides, what about Zane?"

Lauren rolled her eyes. "A girl can look, can't she?"

Chuckling, Sadie swiped her thumb across the screen to unlock her phone.

New evidence. Things have changed. Do NOT leave your apartment until I get there. - Adam

The air seemed to leave the room, and she gasped for breath. The message was typical from Adam. Direct and to the point without even the slightest consideration that she might disobey. The body in the morgue. Someone hunting down and draining the blood of alaras. Two dead so far. Was there another one?

She stumbled to the dining room and sat in one of the chairs.

"Sadie? What's wrong?" Lauren's concerned face filled her vision. Lauren. Her sister. She must be strong because if something happened to Sadie, where would Lauren go? Back to Crofton? Back to the Children of Light?

She forced a smile on her face. "Nothing. I just need to eat. Everything's fine."

Lauren nodded. "Okay," she said, right before snatching Sadie's phone out of her hand. Ignoring Sadie's protests, she tapped in Sadie's code and read the screen.

She looked at Sadie with wide eyes. "This is more serious than I thought," she said. "Who is trying to kill you?"

"No one," Sadie said. "Someone is murdering alara, but there's no specific threat against me."

Lauren handed the phone back to her sister. "I don't think that's true anymore."

Sadie didn't think so either. Heavy footsteps shook her from her thoughts and she glanced up as Tyrell and Brandt walked in.

"Just heard from Adam. We're on lockdown. We're going to finish packing but hold off on loading the truck until he gets here," Tyrell said as Brandt locked the deadbolt behind them. Sadie shuddered and folded her arms around herself. You never realize how good life is until you're in the position where someone might take it away. Then again, she was in the room with two berserkers. Even without their rage, they were extremely deadly. There was no safer place for her to be.

Pushing all thoughts of bloodless bodies and death aside, she busied herself with packing up her apartment, shoving things in any box or bag she could find. She had a feeling that she was never going to see this place again and didn't want to forget anything important. She paused and looked around the room. It was small, but comfortable and had served them well as a cozy barrier from the harsh outside world. While she had never been in the Odinshield apartments, she suspected they were as cold and functional as the rest of the building. If Adam had any role in designing them, it was guaranteed.

Deep voices outside of her bedroom announced Adam's arrival. She shoved the rest of her T-shirts into her backpack and headed into the front room. The room was packed with large masculine bodies as what seemed like the entire Odinshield Protection Agency crowded into her living room, including her newest patient. Judging by the way he moved, his wounds were healing nicely. Erich stood straight, yet his body was guarded like a serpent ready to strike. His black T-shirt hugged his broad shoulders as he crossed his arms over his chest and listened to his brother speak. Lauren sat to the side in one of the dining room chairs, her eyes the size of teacup saucers.

"Sadie. Good, you're done. You should probably hear this," Adam said. The wall of Berserkers parted to allow her passage, her heart racing as she entered the circle. Whether from the upcoming news, or the close proximity to the new berserker, she didn't know. Erich's eyes flicked to her before quickly looking away.

"What's going on, boss?" Ty said, his face uncharacteristically serious.

"Stefen found footage of the recent attack of the alara in the parking garage. This thing that's hunting alara is supernatural."

The men bristled. Some instinctively reaching for their weapons. "What kind of supe?" Wade asked.

Adam shook his head. "I don't know. Something fast. The camera barely registered it when it was moving."

Pale bodies, floral tattoos, and ravaged throats flashed through Sadie's mind. "And the...blood?" Sadie asked. "Did you see what happened to his blood?"

Adam nodded, running his hand over his short hair. "The picture was grainy, but it looked like the supe was sucking the blood from the victim's neck."

Shocked expletives filled the room. Sadie gave a reassuring glance to her sister who was standing outside of the circle, her face paler than usual. Sadie sensed a presence at her side and turned to find Erich had moved to stand right next to her. He looked down at her and gave her a tight smile before turning to his brother.

"What about Sadie? She's alara," he said. Adam looked between Sadie and Erich and frowned.

"Let's get the girls to the compound right away," he said. "Wade, Ty, and Brandt will take them back to Odinshield.

You and I will load what's left into the truck and meet you there."

The men jumped into action, grabbing boxes and bags and hustling out of the apartment. Sadie crossed the room and folded her sister into a big hug. Lauren hugged her back before pulling away.

"Sadie, this is insane. I don't even know what to think about all this," she said, her voice shaky.

"I'm so sorry, Lauren. Once again, my healing power has put us in danger."

Lauren grabbed her hand and gave it a squeeze. "Don't say that. This isn't your fault, just like what our crazy parents did to you wasn't your fault."

Sadie didn't know what to say. On one hand, she agreed with her sister. No child deserved to endure what she had under the rule of her parents, but there was no denying that if she were born without the power to heal, neither of them would be in this position.

"As long as we're together, we will be fine," she said, squeezing Lauren's hand back.

Lauren flushed as Brandt walked by carrying a box. "As long as he's with me, I'll definitely be fine."

Sadie rolled her eyes. "Lauren, can you be serious for one minute? You can't joke around about this."

"Why not?" Lauren asked. "I have to, Sadie, or I'm going to lose my mind. All of this crap is scary as hell. I'd much rather appreciate these handsome men than sit around wringing my hands."

Sadie didn't know what to say. Lauren was right. What good would come from crying and worrying? After all they'd been though, they would handle this, just like they'd always done.

"I get it," Sadie said. "And just so you know, Brandt is single."

She cut off Lauren's excited squeal by adding, "But, he has a past. Getting through his barriers is going to be tough."

"We all have a past," Lauren said.

Sadie couldn't argue that point. With her history, she of all people knew that someone's messed up past didn't mean they couldn't be in a relationship.

"Very true, sis," Sadie said, reaching out to brush a stray strand of hair away from Lauren's face.

Lauren opened her mouth to say something, but stopped, her eyes settling on an object over Sadie's shoulder. Sadie turned and bumped into a hard wall of berserker abs. With a startled cry, she stumbled back but a firm grip on her arms prevented her from falling.

"Whoa, I gotcha," her patient said as he set her upright on her feet. He quickly let go of her arms like his hands were on fire. "Sorry, I was probably standing a little too close."

Sadie gave a small smile. "No, it's not you. I'm just jumpy right now."

Erich nodded but didn't speak. Sadie swallowed hard as his bright blue eyes studied her face, like he was memorizing every detail of her features. They lingered on her lips, before moving back up to her eyes. A small hand waved in between them.

"Hi, I'm Lauren. Sadie's sister."

Sadie giggled, a little embarrassed at being caught staring. Erich recovered quickly, shaking her sister's hand with gentlemanly propriety.

"Erich Birkeland. Adam's brother."

Sadie pointed to Erich's side. "Make sure you don't lift anything heavy. I don't want your cut to open."

Erich smiled. "Yes, ma'am. I'll be sure to only carry the pillows."

Sadie laughed. "It's good to have a patient that actually listens." Erich shrugged and rubbed the back of his neck.

"We're not exactly known for thinking things through."

"You mean, all of you are a bunch of stubborn asses," Sadie said, with a mock frown. Erich tipped his head back and laughed.

"Very true," he said. "Speaking of being an ass, I want to apologize for the way I acted earlier. I don't know what came over me. "

"The berserker rage is hard to control."

"That's just the thing. I wasn't in a rage. I hadn't gone nuclear. I was just..." he held out his hands and shrugged. "Anyway, please trust me when I say you were never in any danger. I would rather die than hurt you."

Sadie studied his earnest features. "You know what? I believe you."

Erich looked relived. "Good," he said. "I'd better get back to moving you out of here. The sooner you get to Odin-shield, the better."

"Thanks for the help," Sadie said. "And remember, pillows only." Erich laughed and gave her a salute before heading into Lauren's bedroom. He soon emerged carrying a large box of textbooks. Sadie sighed. Berserkers never listen.

Lauren turned wide eyes toward her sister. "What was that about?"

"I can't tell you," Sadie said, waving to Wade who was talking to Adam across the living room. "Doctor-patient confidentiality."

Ignoring her sister's protests, Sadie hitched her backpack onto her shoulder and handed Lauren her suitcase.

Wade approached them. "You two ready?"

At Sadie's nod, Wade and Ty led them out of the apartment, Brandt following close behind. Wade gave her a reassuring smile as they held the elevator doors open for them. Sadie and her sister stood in the back of the elevator, behind the wall of berserker bodies.

"Same formation on the way to the SUV. I'll take point. Watch for movement from the sides. I hear these fuckers move fast," Wade said, pulling a knife from his vest holster. Lauren gave a small yelp in fear. Sadie grabbed her hand as they rode the rest of the way in silence. As soon as they left the building, they hurried toward the SUV that was waiting at the curb.

"Get in, princess," Ty said, taking Lauren's suitcase. Sadie and Lauren slid into the backseat, Brandt close behind. Lauren looked like a small child sandwiched in between Sadie and the huge berserker. Tyrell slammed the rear hatch and walked around to the passenger seat.

"Gear is stowed, let's go," he said. Wade pulled the SUV away from the curb, careful to use his turning signal as he slowly merged into traffic. It was the tail end of rush hour, so the roads that were usually congested with cars were beginning to lighten. Wade kept the SUV in the middle lane, traveling at the exact speed limit. Sadie gazed out of the window, expecting to see a nightmarish blur of movement just before something crashed through the SUV window and tore out her throat. She shuddered and turned away. Grabbing her sister's hand, she gave it a squeeze, more to reassure herself than to comfort Lauren.

"I don't want to be a backseat driver, but shouldn't we, you know, get the heck out of here?" Sadie said, panic seeping into her voice.

"The last thing we need is to be pulled over by enforcement. They might make us get out of the car and you'll be exposed," Wade said. He glanced at her in the rearview mirror. "We'll take the long route just in case you are already on the supe's radar and they're following us, but don't worry. We'll be there soon."

As far as Sadie was concerned, it wouldn't be soon enough.

CHAPTER 9

*E*rich shifted the box of textbooks to one arm so he could open the back door to the apartment building. The moving truck was backed into the parking spot a short distance from the door, making the loading process quick and easy. He hopped inside of the truck and set the box down next to some suitcases and a giant stuffed bear. His skin tingled as he looked around at the loaded truck. Sadie's stuff. The scent of lavender hung in the air. His stomach flipped as he ran his hand along her suitcase. Black. Practical. Had she packed it herself? Where was she now?

A noise outside of the truck drew his attention, and he straightened and looked around. No one was there. He turned away and jumped out of the truck. What was she doing to him? Her alara magic had him so obsessed, he was stroking her stuff like a fucking psycho.

Still, it'd be nice if he could have a conversation with her without growling or staring like a lovesick fool. Love? Is it possible to love someone after one day? No, all of that love at first sight bullshit only existed in movies and romance novels. What he felt was different. It was more than attraction and lust. He was meant to provide for and protect Sadie with his life. A compulsion he felt down to the marrow of his bones. He had never met an alara before, maybe this was how everyone felt about them. Maybe, in addition to being able to sense the inner workings of the body, alara, were able to manipulate the mind. Stroke the emotion center to make their work easier when dealing with patients.

"Make room."

Erich snapped out of his deep thoughts and moved to the side to allow that guy with the pale eyes access to the moving van. What was his name? Ben? Bran?

"Hey, you're Bran, right? I saw you earlier today at the clinic."

The guy shoved a box into the truck and turned, eyeing him warily. "Yeah. Name's Brandt," he said.

Erich held out his hand. "I think we started off on the wrong foot. I'm Erich Birkeland. I was here at Odinshield seven years ago."

"I know who you are," Brandt said, ignoring the offered handshake. "Adam's brother."

So the guy's a dick. Fair enough, sometimes berserkers could be a little prickly. Social skills were not high on their priorities. "A lot has changed since I've left. New members," he said, gesturing toward Brandt. "You've renovated the building. Even have a live-in doc."

Brandt stared at him coldly. "That's right," he said.

"How long has Dr. Sadie been with Odinshield?"

Brandt frowned, his grey pupils almost blending into the whites of his eyes. "I think you need to stay away from her before someone gets hurt. Everyone else is okay with you just waltzing in here like some prodigal son, but I'm not going to just roll over while you hurt my family."

Erich crossed his arms and nodded. "The protective vibe. I get it," he said. "But keep in mind that Odinshield was my family long before you arrived." Brandt glared at him before walking back to the apartment building.

Sadie's alara powers had obviously worked their magic on him, as well. Erich frowned as jealousy twisted his gut into knots. Did they have a history? What exactly had Brandt said, and more importantly done, to Sadie? If he was feeling half of what Erich felt, there was a good chance that Brandt had at least attempted to move on her. Has he touched her?

Erich resisted the urge to go upstairs and rip the fucker's arms off. He sighed, scrubbing his face with his hand. If the other guys felt the same way he did, how did Adam keep them from killing each other? He was so on edge, he was about to lose his mind. Not a good thing when that mind belongs to a berserker. Thinking back to all of the women he'd been with, Erich couldn't think of a single one that affected him the way Sadie did. Were all alaras that powerful? If so, the scope of their magic was downright terrifying!

Shaking himself out of his thoughts, Erich headed back up to Sadie's apartment. The sooner his woman, um, Sadie had her stuff, the better. He wanted her comfortable and happy, ideally for the rest of her life.

The three remaining members of Odinshield made quick work of the rest of the necessary household goods. They had all of the boxes loaded into the moving truck and were doing a last-minute sweep of the apartment when Adam's phone beeped. Glancing at the screen, he frowned.

"Everything okay, boss?" Brandt asked. Adam nodded as he put his phone back in his pocket.

"Stefen got a ping off of Jamison's cell phone. He thinks he located him."

"Jamison?" Erich asked.

"The scientist working on the serum. He's been MIA for a few days. With the supplies delayed for a month and our fucking scientist missing, this whole project is turning into a clusterfuck," Adam said. He ran his hand through his short brown hair. "Let's get back to headquarters. I have to deal with this."

"Want me to come along," Erich asked. Before he left Odinshield, he had made sure to know everything that was going on. Between him and Wade, continuity of command was firmly established. If something had happened to Adam, he and Wade could step in and finish the mission with barely a hiccup. He was back but he since he still had one foot out of the door, he wasn't sure about his place in the organization.

Adam checked his watch. "No, head back to HQ and get Sadie moved in. Wade and I will deal with Jamison."

Message received. Still, it wasn't surprising. He couldn't leave for seven years and expect for things to be the same when he returned. Life didn't work that way.

As they exited the apartment building, Adam tossed a set of keys to Erich. "Take Lauren's car back to Odinshield. Brandt, you take Sadie's and I'll drive the truck."

Lauren's keychain had two keys and about twenty pieces of dangly metal jewelry on it. The biggest one, a bright yellow pineapple wearing sunglasses was right next to her vehicle's key fob. Erich pressed the lock button on the key fob to find Lauren's car. Not surprisingly, it was a bright green coupe and had another sunglass-wearing pineapple dangling from the mirror. Getting into the car was challenging, but once he had the seat pulled all of the way back, he was able to fit his body in. Barely. His head still brushed the roof. Hopefully he won't hit any potholes on the way back.

CHAPTER 10

*S*adie gasped as she entered her temporary home. The entrance opened into a large living room, already furnished with soft leather couches and decorated in conservative blues and browns. A full kitchen, stocked with state-of-the-art appliances, stood to the immediate right and the attached dining room opened up into a spacious living area. Two doors stood on opposite ends of the living room, presumably leading to bedrooms. The entire apartment was decorated with coordinating art and plants. It was hard to believe that any member of Odinshield was responsible for designing such a homey place.

"Wow," Lauren said, pulling her suitcase behind her. "I was expecting something like a hotel room."

"Yeah, me too," Sadie said, strolling into the kitchen. She ran her hand over the granite countertop next to the stainless steel double oven. "This is...nice!"

Setting her backpack onto the kitchen counter, she opened the door to the closest bedroom. It was decorated in the same blues and browns as the living room but had accent items of light blue sprinkled about. A queen-size bed stood in the middle of the room and a dresser and vanity sat along the wall. Going further into the room, she noticed that the bathroom led into a large walk-in closet.

"Sadie! I think you need to see this," Lauren called.

Her heart in her throat, Sadie rushed out of the bedroom and into the empty living room. "What is it? What's wrong?"

Lauren peeked her head out of the other bedroom on the opposite of the apartment and grinned. "Just come here," she said.

Taking in a shuddering breath, Sadie strolled across the living room and through the door. She stopped, her jaw dropping open.

"It's nice, isn't it?" Lauren said.

That was an understatement. The bedroom was twice as large as the other one and decorated in light blue, white, and gold. The king-size bed rested on a raised platform and was covered in a luscious white comforter. Sparkling gold lamps sat on white nightstands.

The beautiful bed wasn't the highlight of the room, though. Separated by a grand archway was the largest bathroom she had ever seen. With its large oval tub, glass-enclosed shower and deep double sinks, the bathroom was larger than her entire bedroom back at her apartment.

Lauren came up to her side and gave her a hug. "I think this room is for you, sis."

"No," Sadie said, shaking her head. "I can't stay here. This is so…"

"Much! I know," Lauren said. "But you deserve this. After all you've been through."

Sadie turned to her sister and grasped her hand. "You take it," she said. When Lauren began to protest, she pressed on. "I mean it. You're working so hard in school. You should stay here."

Lauren looked at her as if she had lost her mind. "Are you

serious? You looked out for me while going to college and med school. It's about time you get a little reward for all you've done."

Sadie looked around. All of the symbols of luxury made her uncomfortable. To say her childhood had been unusual was putting it lightly. Growing up, she had shared a room with six other children. She'd only had a small mattress to sleep on and no privacy. Everything she owned was available to the rest of the group. Even her blood had been available for church use.

Cool hands touched her cheeks and moved her head so that she was looking at her sister. Despite having different fathers, they could pass as twins. The stress of school and, you know, hiding from a crazy killer made Lauren's brown eyes stand out against her thin face. When had she gotten so pale? "Stop arguing with me. You deserve this," she said. "Come on, let's get our stuff."

As she followed her sister into the living area, she noticed for the first time the painting on the wall. She stopped and studied it. It depicted a palatial castle nestled against snow-capped mountains. Toward the bottom, a white wolf stood frozen, mid-stride, as it loped toward the tree line. She wasn't sure, but she suspected this was a painting of Wolveshire, the Ulfhednar headquarters. She didn't know exactly where, but she knew it was located far up north. Squinting at the signature on the bottom right, she could barely make out a S and a N. Brandt. Who knew he was so talented?

"Coming through," a deep voice said, drawing her attention away from the painting. Lauren jumped to the side as Tyrell and Erich carried the Great Big Boil into the room.

"Where do you want this?" Erich asked. Lauren skipped further into the room.

"Right here in the middle, in front of the TV," Lauren said.

Sadie scurried into the kitchen to get out of the way. She cringed as they moved the nice leather love seat into the hallway and shoved Lauren's couch in its place. Lauren gave a dramatic sigh as she collapsed onto its soft cushions.

"Well, she's happy," Erich said, leaning against the kitchen counter and folding his arms. He glanced at her. "How about you? You okay?"

Sadie pasted a smile on her face. "Me? Yeah, this is great," she said, nodding.

Erich studied her face, his blue eyes not seeming to miss a single detail. "You're safe here," he said, his voice soft and intimate. "I won't let anything happen to you."

He cleared his throat and looked around. "I mean, Odinshield won't let anything happen to you. This place is a fortress."

Sadie didn't have to use her powers to determine Erich's vitals. The slight flush on his cheeks told her everything she needed to know. She smiled, this time a genuine one. "I know. I'm thankful to have your protection," she said. She nudged him with her elbow. "Odinshield's protection, that is."

Erich grinned wide, showing even white teeth. She hadn't noticed it before, but he had an amazing smile. He had the type of smile that was contagious, like he was spreading his happiness to the rest of the world. She grinned and ducked her head.

"No, ma'am," he said, lifting her head up with a gentle finger under her chin. "There is no hiding your feelings around me. Odinshield rules."

Sadie blushed. "Everyone hides a little bit of themselves."

"Not me," Erich said. He held his arms wide, exposing his chest. "I'm an open book."

Sadie raised an eyebrow.

Erich chuckled. "I'm serious. Ask me anything."

"Okay," Sadie said. "Do you have a girlfriend?"

"Nope."

"Why not?"

Erich shrugged. "Nothing has ever lasted long enough."

"Why did you leave Odinshield?"

"Not enough pretty girls," Erich said. He smiled at her. "But I see that has changed."

Sadie blushed. It was probably best to change the subject. "So this is my life, I guess."

"It's not so bad," Erich said. "Cafeteria's open 24/7. The gym has state-of-the-art equipment." Erich shrugged. "What else do you need?"

"I don't want to sound ungrateful." Sadie spread her arms to encompass the apartment. "This place is amazing. I am so thankful that Adam has allowed us to stay here."

"So am I," Erich said.

"It's just..." Sadie sighed. "I'm used to being independent and making my own decisions. Now...am I going to live the rest of my life here? Can I never leave without fear that some monster will kill me?"

She had spent her childhood restricted and controlled. Although she wasn't a prisoner here, a small part of her couldn't help but feel like she had gone right back to where she'd started.

"We'll find what's killing alara. That's what we do." Erich hesitated before adding. "Hey, if you ever want to leave, just let me know. I'll take you wherever you want to go. Just say the word."

Sadie could take comfort in that, at least. Although she was sequestered within the walls of Odinshield, she wouldn't be a prisoner. Then again, even before alara started getting murdered, she had rarely gone anywhere except for trips to the morgue or Jamison's lab. Fun times.

"As much as I hate to admit it, my work is my whole life. I go to work and come home. That's it."

"Really? I find it hard to believe you don't have guys beating down your door for a date," Erich said.

Sadie blushed. "No, nothing like that. Between patching you guys up and working on Adam's serum, I don't have time for much else."

Erich sighed and leaned against the counter. "That damn serum. I can't believe Adam is trying to replicate that. The last time he used it, it didn't end well."

That was an understatement. Sadie had read about Adam and Wade's time in the protective force and the toll that Project Redwood had taken on their bodies and mind.

They had spent months testing different concoctions in the hope of being able to control their berserker rage. The side effects had been extensive. After all these years, Adam still had migraines and lacked feeling in his right tricep, the injection site for one of the more successful versions of the serum. It's that version he was trying to replicate, only without the muscle numbness and suicidal ideation.

"He thinks it can be done," Sadie said. "Without the terrible side effects, of course."

"I just don't understand why he is so hell-bent on this. I've never seen anyone control their rage as good as him."

Sadie looked at him. "Maybe the serum is not for him," she said softly.

Erich looked away, his eyes thoughtful. "Well, I know for sure, I'm not taking it." At Sadie's surprised look, he shrugged. "Sometimes it's a curse, but I am what I am. I'm not going to let some scientist change that."

He was probably right. Sadie hadn't known him when he was part of Odinshield, but most of the guys could handle themselves in a fight even without using their berserker rage. Well, besides Stefen who, even with all of the training, was still unable to control his rage. As a result, he rarely left the compound.

"I understand," Sadie said. Erich looked relieved, like her opinion of him was important. "I used to think being an alara was a curse." At Erich's shocked look, she gave him a small smile.

"My childhood was…unique. I wanted nothing more than to be a normal person."

A loud bang made her jump. She spun around to find Tyrell standing with his hands on his hips, a large box at his feet. "Well," he said, wiping his brow mockingly. "I'm so glad I could do all of the heavy lifting so that your royal highness could stand around chatting."

Sadie felt her face turn hot. "Oh…I'm—"

"Not you," Tyrell said. He pointed at Erich. "I'm talking to Sleeping Beauty over there."

Sadie suppressed her grin as Tyrell stalked off, grumbling to herself. She turned to Erich.

"Um…I think you'd better go," she said. Erich smiled, rubbing his short hair sheepishly.

"Yeah, that's probably a good idea," he said. He walked to the edge of the kitchen before turning back. "Hey, I meant it when I said I'll take you somewhere. Anywhere you want to go. Just let me know."

"I will. Thank you," Sadie said. He grinned at her before leaving the apartment, his long legs cutting the distance in just a few strides. Standing at five foot eight inches, she was tall for a woman, but when she stood next to Erich, she felt like a dainty porcelain doll in need of protecting. It was a new feeling.

She stayed in the kitchen as the men carried in boxes and bags. They worked quickly, seeming to relish the heavy lifting. Before long, they were gone, calling out their goodbyes as they left the apartment. Sadie moved to the leather recliner and sighed.

"I guess this is real," Lauren said as she lay sprawled on the Great Big Boil.

"Yep," Sadie said. She leaned back and stared at the ceiling. In the span of one day, she'd learned that she was being hunted, met the most handsome man she'd ever seen, and moved herself and her sister into the compound. Strangely enough, as far as crazy days went, this wasn't even in the top five.

CHAPTER 11

*E*rich's eyes snapped open. He didn't have to check the clock to know the time. 0600. During his time in the protective force, he had trained his body to wake first thing in the morning and be ready to go at a moment's notice. Even after he had resigned from the force, he had retained the habit.

It was nice getting up before the rest of the world had a chance to piss him off.

After throwing on some shorts and a T-shirt, he rode the elevator down to the third floor. Half of the entire floor consisted of a state-of-the-art gym, complete with sauna and a lap pool. The other half held a pretty amazing lounge area, complete with pool table and movie theater. Erich hadn't had a chance to really explore the place until now.

When he had first joined Odinshield, back when the group was just standing up, they had only owned one half of the second floor. Space was tight, but it had been enough at the time. With the Head Council's guidance, they had put a small dent into the scourge of supernatural mischief that had plagued Triton City.

Odinshield had been a test. For centuries, Ulfhednar berserkers had lived in the northern country, learning how to control their rage and hone their skills. As tales of supernatural crimes reached their icy fortress, teams would be dispatched to eliminate the menace. That seemed to work until the slaughter of an entire pack of were-shifters put the entire city on high alert. A thorough investigation revealed that an underlying war between the shifter pack and a rogue clan of berserkers had erupted into a blood bath. The resulting carnage wasn't pretty.

Complaints from the remaining packs, and even from other supernatural species prompted the Head Council to create a field office right in the city. Odinshield Protection Agency had a humble beginning, but judging by the look of things, business was booming.

The elevator doors opened, almost silent except for the soft ding it made to announce the end of its journey. Erich turned left toward the gym. Despite the lingering prain in his side, he was ready to get back into fighting shape. Luckily, his knee felt surprisingly pain-free. His kind tended to recover quickly, but he was a bit surprised with how fast he was healing.

He pushed his way into the gym. Free weights were to his immediate right, in front of the mirror in case someone wanted to admire their form while lifting. Directly in front of him sat multiple types of cardio machines and to his left sat rows of weight lifting machines. A quick investigation of the back rooms revealed a stretching area, a meditation room, and a small break room with a fridge fully stocked with energy drinks, vitamin water from the mountains of Sardova, and snacks.

Erich eyed the meditation room and rubbed his shoulder. His thoughts turned to Sadie. Not only was she beautiful, but the sense of peace and calm he felt whenever he was near her was unlike anything he had ever experienced. It's like he had drunk a bottle of whisky and gotten a massage at the same time. But as soon as he was away from her, all of the normal feelings had come crashing into him, full force.

Yeah, he should probably resume the mandatory meditation hour that all members of the Ulfhednar were required to do. He hadn't felt this on edge since his berserker rage first manifested itself when he was seventeen. As he walked toward the meditation room, his phone buzzed.

We have an assignment. I want you on it. Meeting in the conf room in 10. - Wade

Erich sighed. Change of plans. He glanced at the cardio equipment. He could at least get in a couple of miles before he headed up.

Legs pumping in line with the treadmill's track, Erich psyched himself up for the mission. He didn't have to know the details to know that they were about to deal with an asshole of a supe that couldn't keep its hands to itself. During his time on the outside, he had lost track of the Frelshednar's activities, but if they were still as chaotic and undisciplined as before, they were probably the perpetrator.

He turned up the treadmill's speed with the hopes of fitting in three miles. If he was in his prime, he could do it, no problem, but he was out of shape for an Ulfhednar. With only ten minutes available, it looked like he was only going to be able run two miles.

With a sigh, he turned off the machine and wiped it down. Grabbing a water from the break room, he headed toward the elevator and upstairs to the penthouse suite.

Wade had already arrived when he walked into the conference room. He seemed deep in thought as he tapped on a laptop, not even noticing when Erich sat across from him and cleared his throat.

"So...we're going into the field tonight?"

Wade looked up, startled. Erich narrowed his eyes. It was rare for Wade to let down his guard, even within the protective walls of Odinshield. He gestured toward Wade's laptop.

"What are you working on?"

Wade closed the laptop with a click and sat back in his chair. "Just some business with the local coven. And to answer your question, we're not just going out tonight. Our target is a nocturnal creature. We're going to prepare and set up some surveillance while it's in its hole."

Erich took a sip of his water. "Okay, why? What did it do?"

"Let's wait for the others to arrive." Wade looked at his watch.

"Hey, when do I get one of those?" Erich said, tapping his wrist.

Wade shrugged. "If you're going to stay for good, Stefen should have given you one by now. I guess with all of this business with the doc, things fell through the cracks."

"Tell me about it," Erich said. "I don't know how you can focus with her around."

"The doc's cute, but I wouldn't say I'm distracted."

Erich chuckled. "No, I mean with her being an alara and all."

At Wade's blank look, Erich continued. "You know, how you feel super protective. Like you'll die for her and stab yourself in your own heart if she asked it of you."

Wade blinked. "Wow, Erich. Who knew you were so poetic."

"You know what I mean."

Wade nodded. "That's how you feel about the doc?"

"Yeah. Because she's alara."

The silence in the room stretched to such an uncomfortable level that Erich started to tense under Wade's unceasing stare. "What, man?"

Wade sighed. "Listen, I like the doc and all, but there's nothing beyond that."

Before Erich could respond, Brandt walked in and dropped into the chair closest to the door.

"It's a bit early for a meeting, Wade," he grumbled. He looked like he had ended up on the wrong side of a train wreck as he glared at Wade with bloodshot eyes.

"Good morning to you, too, sunshine," Wade said.

"Cut the crap," Brandt said, rubbing his face. "I haven't had coffee yet and I'm not in the mood."

"When are you ever in the mood?" Ty said, walking through the door with a Coffee Bean cup in his hand. He sat on the opposite side of the table and took a sip of his coffee, chuckling at Brandt's envious look. "Want a sip?" he asked, with a wink.

Wade opened his laptop and rapidly typed on the keys. The lights dimmed and the projector in the ceiling hummed to life.

"Our client is Leslie Lockhart of the Deer Creek shifters," Wade said. A picture of a petite, middle-aged woman flashed onto the screen.

"Deer Creek," Erich said. "Deer shifters?"

"Fox," Wade said. "I know, it doesn't make sense. Anyway, she is due to arrive in town later on today and her clan wants us to escort her from the station to her house."

"Why?" Brandt asked. Wade pressed a button and Leslie's picture was replaced with a picture of a large black dog. Its head was turned toward the camera, red eyes glowing, and its mouth was open as if caught in mid snarl.

"Gwyllgi. The Dog of Darkness. It's been sighted walking the streets for the past couple of nights. The fox-shifters are understandably concerned."

"Why don't we just call the werewolves and ask them to get rid of their cousin?" Ty said, taking an audible sip of his coffee. He flashed a grin at Brandt and chuckled at the middle finger that greeted him.

"I agree that this is below our pay grade, but it's a good mission to get Erich back into the swing of things," Wade said.

Brandt scrubbed his face with his hand and sighed. "Okay, fine. But why do you need four of us for an escort op? You and Erich should be able to get the little fox home in one piece."

Wade pressed a button on the keyboard and sat back. Erich studied the grainy screenshot taken from a surveillance feed. The picture was of a nondescript road. Pavement. Road lines. Tall grass and bushes sat along the sides of the road.

"What am I looking at?" Erich asked.

Wade picked up the laser pointer and pointed to the bottom left of the screen. "Right here."

Erich leaned forward and studied the area. A tall dark blur blended into the background bushes. If Wade hadn't pointed it out, he would have missed it.

Another tap on the keyboard brought up the actual video feed. "Stefen has been monitoring the surveillance feeds along the road from the station to Leslie's house. So far, he hasn't seen any Gwyllgi, but he did see this. Watch."

The video started with a broad shot of the road. Erich's eye immediately went to the bottom left corner of the screen. The man-sized shadow was not there yet.

"Keep your eyes on the bottom of the video," Wade said, just as a blur shot across the screen. Just as quickly, it stopped and the dark form appeared in front of the bushes. It was tall, though the perspective could be off, depending on where the camera was sitting. The dark form turned to the side and tilted its head back as if it was smelling the air. Just as quickly as it appeared, it disappeared offscreen."

"That was the same type of supe that we saw in the

parking garage video," Erich said. "This shifter. Is she an alara?"

Wade turned off the presentation and turned on the lights. "Yup. That's why I want four of us. Erich and I will be on escort duty. I want Ty and Brandt running surveillance ops. Keep an eye on the house and the route. These fuckers move fast, so we're going to need intel as soon as possible."

"What are we looking for, a dog or a man?" Ty asked.

"Both."

Brandt yawned. "Fine. But that still doesn't explain why you called a meeting at the ass-crack of dawn."

Wade stood and tucked his laptop under his arm. "Go eat your Wheaties, or whatever you do in the morning. But I want the two of you to scout out the route and set up better surveillance so that Stefen can monitor the entire op."

Erich stayed behind while the rest of the guys left the room. He hadn't been on an op for seven years and wasn't sure how he felt about it. While he was determined to find the monster that was killing alara, going on an official op felt like the point of no return. The moment he strapped on his weapons, he would be an official member of Odinshield again. He'd be back to fighting the endless battle between protecting the innocent and unsuspecting from the dregs of supernatural society. It's an honorable mission, but never-ending. No matter how many criminals they put into the ground, more will always spring up. There will always be an innocent in need of protection. His mind flashed to Sadie. Honey brown hair and deep beautiful brown eyes. Plump lips, slightly parted.

His Sadie. His innocent in need of protecting. And there were millions more just like her.

His berserker rage was both a gift and a curse. But if he didn't use it to protect the innocent, then what was he? What was his purpose? To murder and fuck like the Frelshednar?

To eventually become one of the honor-less supes that the Ulfhednar hunts down?

Grabbing his empty water bottle, Erich strode out of the room. He needed to eat and take a shower, in that order. But first, he had to see a man about a watch.

CHAPTER 12

*C*ursing under her breath, Sadie tossed her cell phone into her bag. It had been months since she'd heard from Jamison, the head scientist that Adam had contracted to work on his serum. Adam wasn't happy that he was MIA, which meant Sadie wasn't happy, either.

"Everything alright?"

Sadie jumped, her hand clutching her chest. Lauren was lounging on the Great Big Boil, eating a bowl of cereal. Sadie had been so deep in thought, she hadn't noticed her sister sitting there.

"You scared me," Sadie said with a nervous laugh. "I thought you had class right now."

Lauren set her bowl down on the coffee table. "I'm skipping it."

Sadie frowned. Lauren was as studious as Sadie had been in school. Skipping class was usually out of the question. "Are you sick?"

Lauren pursed her lips and fixed Sadie with a hard stare. "No, that's not it."

Sadie crossed the room and placed her palm on Lauren's

forehead. Temperature was normal, no other anomalies that she could detect. It was only when Sadie stepped back that she noticed Lauren's fierce glare.

"Is everything alright?" she asked.

Lauren held up her arm. "See this?"

Sadie frowned. "You're arm?"

"The watch," Lauren snapped. Sadie hadn't noticed it at first, but Lauren was wearing one of the smartwatches that were standard issue for Odinshield's inner circle. "Do you know what this does?"

"Of course," Sadie said. "I have my own."

"How interesting," Lauren said. She glanced at hers. "Ty dropped this off this morning. Apparently, this thing locks and unlocks our doors."

Sadie nodded. "Yes, they all do but only ours should unlock our door, so you don't have to worry— "

"He also said that it's linked to your expense account," Lauren said, glaring at her.

Sadie's stomach clenched. "Oh...He said that?"

"Oh yes," Lauren said with an exaggerated nod. "Not knowing about any expense account, I naturally asked him about it."

Sadie closed her eyes and cursed. "I wanted to tell you— "

"Tell me what? That you have been sitting on a pile of money while I work double shifts?"

"I couldn't tell you. I had to sign an NDA before I could take the job."

"I get it. This whole place seems very special ops. Top secret crap. But you didn't have to let me kill myself trying to help pay the bills."

"I know."

"You're a doctor! Even without the expense account, you would have made enough to support us."

"You're right."

"Stop agreeing with me!" Lauren shouted. She jumped off of the couch and pointed a finger at Sadie's chest. "Stop it!"

Sadie held out her hands. "I'm sorry. What do you want me to say? I'm agreeing with you because you ARE right."

Lauren threw her hands up with a gasp of exasperation. "You are so annoying when you do that."

Sadie pressed her lips together in a tight smile, holding back the words that threatened to bubble out of her throat. Lauren was right, of course. Sadie had made a huge mistake in keeping her new salary a secret. At the time, she had thought she was doing the right thing. Her position at Odinshield was new and seemed kind of tenuous. Berserkers rarely got hurt and healed quickly, so why did they need a doctor?

Once she had the chance to see the guys in action and witness the beatings they put their bodies through, she recognized the need for her skills. By then, it had been too late. The lie had been told and they were happily living well below their means.

Sadie had held on to the lie, though, precisely to avoid this very situation. She should have told Lauren the truth from the very beginning. Hearing about her salary from someone else made this ten times worse.

Sadie closed the distance between them and threw her arms around her sister. "I'm so sorry for lying to you. If I could do it again, I would change everything."

Lauren didn't return the hug, holding her body stiffly as if she was only tolerating her sisters touch. With a soft sniffle, Sadie stepped away. She hated the dead look in Lauren's eyes, as if she no longer had any fight in her.

"Please let me explain."

Without a word, Lauren turned and collapsed on the Great Big Boil. Crossing her arms, she fixated on a spot on the far wall. Sadie took that as permission.

"When I first got this job, it was a dream come true, but I didn't think it would last. These guys are so big and strong, why would they need a doctor?"

Lauren frowned. "Why wouldn't they. Muscles don't stop knives."

Sadie swallowed hard. They were getting into NDA territory here, but the last thing she wanted to do was lie to her sister again. Besides, because of this new, crazy supernatural, Lauren's life had been turned upside down and she was literally being protected by Odinshield. She deserved to know what was going on around her.

Sadie hoped that Adam would agree.

She sat in the recliner adjacent to Lauren. "You have to promise not to tell anyone what I'm about to tell you." Lauren's eyes widened and she nodded.

"There are other things out there that are not human. Bad things. Evil things."

"Like wolves?" Lauren said, confusion putting a slight wrinkle between her eyes. "I mean, they can be bad. I wouldn't call them evil though…"

"Worse than wolves, monster type things. There are things that can look like a human, but then change their shape so that they have the features and mannerism of an animal. There are monsters that feed off of human blood and flesh."

Lauren sat back and smirked. "Wow, I expected you to come up with a lie to get you out of this, but this is a reach."

"Think about it! Think about me? I am an alara. If I can exist, how far-fetched is it that monsters can, too?"

"That's different, Sadie," Lauren said. "Yes, you're an alara, but that's normal. You have a gift. Just like some people have photographic memories or are musical geniuses. You're not a monster!"

Sadie leaned back with a sigh. Lauren was being purposefully obtuse, but then again, asking her to believe in monsters was a little far-fetched. To be honest, she hadn't truly believed until Wade had come out of the field with his arm shredded by a Wendigo. Showing Lauren physical proof would end this conversation in a matter of seconds, but Sadie had already said too much. She doubted Adam would forgive her for showing Lauren classified documents.

"I need to tell you the true reason we moved into Odinshield," Sadie said.

"So it wasn't because you were receiving death threats? Another lie?"

"Actually, that's true, but there's more to the story. The man that's killing alara is a supernatural. We don't know what it is, but it's hunting them down and draining their blood."

Lauren paled. "Goodness, Sadie. Why didn't you tell me?"

"I did. Sort of."

"So what if the monster comes here? I know we have these security watches, but stuff like that can be hacked. Or if it's a monster, can't it just break through a window or something?"

"One thing I haven't lied about is Odinshield's true mission. It really is a protection agency. These guys know what they're doing."

"Okay, sure. But how can they stop a supernatural being?"

Sadie hesitated. This was the second secret that she was going to reveal. By breaking the NDA, Adam had the right to fire her. He could toss them both out on the street, even with a deadly supernatural after her blood. Yet the guilt of lying to her sister still pressed down on her. Lauren had been through so much. She deserved to know the truth about the world around her.

"The guys here are not normal men. They're not human," Sadie said. A part of her wanted Lauren to accept that explanation and move on, but judging by the look on her face, that wasn't going to happen.

"So what are they?" Lauren asked. A very simple question. Logical.

By answering, Sadie was putting both of their futures in question.

"They...they're berserkers. They're supernatural."

Lauren was silent for a second, her head lightly nodding as if taking a lot of information in at once. Sadie paused, giving her a chance to accept the news.

"So what is a berserker? Guys who go berserk?" Lauren smirked.

Sadie let out a deep breath she hadn't even been aware she was holding. "Well, yeah. Kind of. Berserkers have the potential to be very deadly once their powers are triggered. With their elevated senses and supernatural speed, they can be quite effective in a fight."

"Berserker," Lauren said, as if trying the word out to see how she liked it. "I can see that. There's something off about these guys. Like, I know they're tough and stuff, but they seem...ultra. The way they move and talk to each other. It's like they are trying to hold in an explosion."

Sadie nodded. "That's the training. Once their berserker gene is awakened, they go through strict training to learn how to control their rage."

Lauren lifted an eyebrow. "Rage? I thought we could trust these guys."

Sadie placed a hand on Lauren's arm. "We can. You can trust any of these guys with your life. But not all berserkers are like them. Berserkers are stronger and faster than humans. Their senses are enhanced, so they can see, smell and hear better than us. They also heal faster. But they have a weakness."

"Rage," Lauren said.

"Yep. An untrained berserker can go from calm to out of control in a split second, and when he is enraged, he will kill everything in his path. Friend or foe."

Lauren leaned back. "You're not making a case for trusting them."

Sadie sighed. "The Odinshield guys are different. They're Ulfhednar. They're trained to harness their rage so that it *works for* them instead of controlling them. When a berserker is enraged, he's ten times stronger and faster than when he's in his natural state. Ulfhednar have learned how to benefit from that while still keeping a level head. That's what makes them so much more powerful than other berserkers."

"So what if they fail and rage out? Nobody's perfect."

Sadie's mind flashed to Stefen. The lone Ulfhednar who never could learn to harness his rage. "Some are better at it than others, but most of the guys here are experts. The cream of the crop. You will never see them out of control."

"Most?"

"Well, there is one. Stefen. But he is contained in a secure floor of the building. You will never cross paths without another berserker with him."

"Great," Lauren said, sarcasm dripping from her voice.

"The point is, this thing goes deeper than I originally let on. I should have told you about my salary. Now that I think about it, there was no excuse to keep you in the dark."

"I agree," Lauren said. "I was so stressed out trying to work and go to school. I can't believe you sat back on a big wad of cash and watched me suffer."

Sadie didn't respond. There was really nothing to say. No defense for her actions. All she could do now was figure out a way to make amends. The twinkle in Lauren's eye caught her off guard.

"There's a way you can make it up to me, though," she said.

Relief flooded through Sadie. Usually, she found her sister's brattiness annoying, but at this moment, seeing Lauren go back to her normal self made her want to celebrate.

"How?" Sadie was careful to keep her tone level. She didn't want to assume that she was forgiven too early and negate the awful thing she had done.

Lauren studied her nails. "I've been eyeing the new XTZ coup for the last month or so. My car is so old and it doesn't even connect to my phone wirelessly."

Sadie almost laughed out loud in joy. If buying her sister a new car meant she was forgiven, she'd buy her ten. With a blood-sucking supernatural hunting her down, the last thing she wanted was for the two of them to be at odds. Especially since it was her fault. Sadie jumped up and embraced her sister, balancing herself with her hand as she sunk deep into the couch cushions.

"Deal!"

CHAPTER 13

The road to Deer Creek was dark and winding. As the SUV cut through the darkness, the inky air temporarily parted to allow the massive vehicle passage, only to snap shut behind it.

With the moon hidden behind clouds, the view outside of the window was pitch black. There may as well had been a canvas over the window. Calling on his power, Erich enhanced his vision. His eyes shown like two golden pinpoints in the reflection of the window. He quickly scanned the countryside before turning off the enhancement. As if a giant SUV wasn't enough to tip off the bad guys, the golden glow of his eyes would scream supernatural.

"No streetlights," Wade said, his hands at a steady ten and two in the steering wheel. "How do you normally drive out here?"

"Foxes have no need for lights." The voice was as small and thin as its owner. Leslie Lockhart, alpha of the Deer Creek fox clan, sat in the back seat next to Erich. She couldn't have been over five feet tall, yet the spark in her eyes radiated command presence. She knew what she wanted and was used to getting her way.

As long as she paid, the men were happy to comply.

The SUV was silent as Wade turned into a gravel driveway that was blocked by a rusty looking gate. A tall lanky man stood to the side of it.

"Don't mind him, he'll let you in," Leslie said.

Wade pulled up and rolled the window down. The man approached the SUV. "Can I help you?"

"Odinshield Protection Agency," Wade said. The man peered into the back of the SUV. His face lit up when he saw Leslie and he gave a nod.

"Come on in," he said, punching a code into the metal box by the gate.

They passed through two other gates, each time being met with a Deer Creek shifter and only being let through once the man saw Leslie.

"It looks like you have good security here," Erich said.

"My boys want to keep me safe," Leslie said. "They can handle most things, but with the new supernatural running around killing alara, they don't want to take the risk."

Wade glanced at her through the rearview mirror. "How did you hear about that? We've been trying to keep it close hold."

Leslie smiled. "We have our contacts, just like you."

The SUV grew silent as Wade pulled in front of a large, palatial house. More shifters stood around the perimeter, most carrying machetes and knives. Ty and Brandt approached when the car stopped.

Erich got out and looked around. The area was quiet, only the soft sound of boots stepping on grass interrupted the sound of the natural surrounding forest.

"Any trouble?" Wade asked.

"Nope. It's been silent. We've been watching the roads for

the last couple of hours. No Gwyllgi and no sign of the supe from the video."

Two shifters removed the matriarch's luggage from the rear hatch and carried them into the house. A short stocky man with shockingly red-hair approached her door. Erich took one last look around before opening it.

"Welcome home, Les," he said, his weathered face breaking into a genuine smile. Leslie slid across the seat and was just about to step out when the red haired man cried out. His body jerked and flailed grotesquely before falling to the ground. Erich pushed the shifter matriarch into the SUV and slammed it closed. He pulled his knife but only saw the slightest blur and then nothing. Wade was next to him in an instant, a knife in hand.

"Ty, Brandt, secure the other side," he ordered, locking the vehicle.

The shifter guards called out orders as they searched the perimeter, some of them shifting right out of their clothes and loping into the forest in order to take advantage of the superior sight, smell, and hearing of a fox. The berserkers stayed where they were, backs to the SUV, eyes glowing as they searched for anything out of the ordinary. A fox growled somewhere in the forest and then yelped in pain. Inside the SUV, Leslie sobbed.

"Jim?" A stout, bearded shifter called out, peering into the forest where the fox was last seen. The rest of the shifters were silent, listening for any sign of life.

"Panama," Wade whispered. The Odinshield men gave soft whistles to acknowledge the order. Eyes still scanning the area, Wade motioned for the nearest shifter to come closer.

"How secure is the house?"

"It's a fortress," the shifter said.

"A fortress with windows?" Erich asked.

The shifter shook his head. "Those are glass-clad polycarbonate. Walls are filled with fiberglass panels. Nothing is getting through them."

Erich lifted his eyebrows, impressed. A sharp knock on the SUV window drew their attention. Erich caught Wade's eye, silently communicating the need for him to watch his back. At Wade's nod, Erich half turned his body toward the SUV. Even with his elevated senses, he could barely make out Leslie's face behind the dark tint, but he could hear her clearly.

"Is he alright?" Leslie asked, her voice thick with emotion. Erich glanced at the body of the red hair shifter. He could almost look like he was sleeping except for the gash in his throat and the blood soaking into the grass. Erich shook his head.

"We need to get you into the house. Stay put until we say so." Leslie hesitated before giving a small nod.

A sharp cry drew his attention. Across the yard, a shifter sank to his knees, his hands clutching his neck, as if to hold back the blood that was seeping between his fingers. Another shifter ran to him and carried him into the house.

"We have to get her out of here," Erich said. "This is going to be a blood bath."

Wade nodded. "Erich, Ty, go."

Erich and Ty spread out, both running toward opposite ends of the tree line. He opened his senses, almost becoming overwhelmed by the competing sounds of the forest and the random sounds from the remaining shifters. He ignored them all, searching for anything out of the ordinary.

The attack came suddenly from the left. Erich managed to get his arm up just in time to deflect it. He hissed as sharp claws ripped into the skin of his arm. On instinct, he shot out his hand, but only grabbed air. Heart pounding, he bushed the berserker rage down, only allowing himself to use the strength and speed of his berserker.

He felt the air shift to his right. He spun, calling on all of his berserker power in the move, and clipped something solid. The supe cried out as it crashed to the ground. Erich followed through with a kick to its abdomen, knocking the supe twenty yards into the forest. Unable to contain himself, Erich shot his head back and roared.

Ty was at his side in an instant. His eyes glowed gold as he scanned the area before shooting off in the supe's direction. Erich followed, sprinting toward the pained moans. While Ty was a master at many fighting styles, Erich had the gift of speed. They arrived at the same time, both men falling onto the supe.

The supe looked like a human and could easily pass as a civilian man. Its black hair was longer than normal and hung messily in front of its face. Red eyes peeked from beneath the greasy locks. It opened its mouth and hissed at them, it's teeth long and sharp like a werewolf.

Erich lifted him, but before he could pin him to the nearby tree, the supe wrenched himself out of his grip. Erich grabbed at him but it had disappeared. Erich saw the blur just as it reached Ty. Before he could call out a warning, Ty grunted, clutching his shoulder. He spun and shot out a foot, catching the supe in the stomach. The supe flew backward but landed deftly on his feet. He grinned at them, a small trickle of blood escaped his bloody lip. Erich frowned. The supe's teeth were not like anything he'd ever seen. The two incisors were long and pointed, like a were shifter, but the rest of his teeth crowded his mouth and ended in sharp points.

"I finally meet worthy opponents," the supe said, brushing a wayward lock of his black hair back in place. "You fight like the Bashar, but your eyes glow gold. What are you?"

"Why are you killing alara," Erich demanded. The supe licked at the blood along the corner of his mouth.

"Why not?" The supe said. "They taste delicious." Sadie's face flashed in Erich's mind. His vision swam as his rage threatened to overtake him. As if sensing his distress, Ty stepped forward, making brief eye contact before shaking his head. Erich took a deep breath. He had to stay on mission, and that meant keeping this asshole talking.

"Sure, whatever," Ty said, sounding bored. "What are you, a kappa?" The supe's jaw snapped shut and his eyes flashed in anger. Being compared to a monstrous cross between a turtle and monkey wasn't the most flattering of things. Ty grinned.

Without warning, the supe launched at Ty, becoming practically invisible, even to the berserker eye. Ty stepped to the right, rolling away from the supe's deadly nails and followed with a jab. He only hit air. The trio fell into a dance of punches and dodges as Erich and Ty tried to take the supe down. Noticing movement to his right, Erich swung. Once again, he only served to move the air around, but a loud shriek told him something hit home. The supe skidded to a halt, a knife wedged deep into his knee. Two more knives quickly found purchase in his back, right in the center where his heart should be. The supe reached behind and pulled out the knives just as Wade appeared next to a tree. He took a couple of steps forward, pulled another knife from his vest and flicked it toward the supe. The supe moved to the side, his movements so fast he once again became nothing but a blur against the background of the forest. Erich frowned. He had only seen one other person move that fast and that was Wade when he was using the gift of the Mtezi, a power possessed only by males with Mti lineage.

"Wade, can you track him?" Erich called out. Wade was already running toward the nearest tree. He placed his palm on the rough bark and disappeared. Erich and Ty stood in silence, their eyes darting back and forth, trying to catch sight of either of them. Brandt ran into the clearing, startling the men. Erich quickly signaled for him to be quiet and alert. It wasn't long before Wade reappeared about twenty feet away.

"The supe's gone," he said, sheathing a small blade back into his vest. "I managed to hit him one more time, but I couldn't take him down."

Ty rubbed his shoulder. "What the fuck was that?"

"I don't know," Wade said. "I've never seen anything like it."

"He's fast, like you," Erich said. "Could he be Mtezi?"

Wade shook his head. "He was fast but he wasn't using the trees to move."

"He mentioned the Bashar. My memory is fuzzy, but they are long gone, right."

Wade turned and walked toward the main house. "We'll bring Stefen into the debrief."

Erich thought back to the first time he had met the technology master. Sure, he seemed quite knowledgeable about computers and the technical side of things, but why he would be involved in a discussion about ancient history was beyond him.

Erich leaned back and released a breath. After Stefen's enthusiastic and extremely thorough briefing on the history of the Bashar, he knew more than he ever wanted to know about the extinct organization. He had underestimated the man. With only an hour's notice, Stefen had whipped together an hour-long dissertation on the origin, mission, and eventual downfall of the supernatural assassins. Even now, he was discussing the hierarchy of the organization with Wade, his arms gesticulating wildly as he made his point.

"Well, that was enlightening," Erich said, turning toward Adam. His brother rubbed his eyes before giving him a weary look.

"Now I remember why I hated school."

"Same," Erich said. "He's a little more…intelligent than the average berserker." Berserkers came in all types, but they tended to be more muscle than brains.

Adam shot a quick glance at the front of the conference room and lowered his voice. "He's a genius," he said. "He was training as an intellect at the Sardovian Academy and on track to be a Precept until the berserker gene came out. He snapped and almost killed a professor. They wanted to execute him, but the Ulfhednar stepped in and convinced them that banishment was better option. A large donation helped things along. Needless to say, he's not welcome back."

"Hence his assignment here," Erich said. "Well, we're lucky to have him."

Adam nodded. "True. He still can't control his rage, though. I don't know if he ever will."

Erich looked at Stefen, who was now going into the details of the Bashar's fighting apparel. Although Erich was currently a reluctant guest at Odinshield, he knew that if he wanted to, he could walk out the front door and never come back. His seven years on the outside had proven that he could handle his rage and live a normal life. As long as no one tried to kill him, that is.

Stefen, on the other hand was a true prisoner. His lack of control meant he couldn't be trusted out in society. Any other berserker would have been executed by Wolveshire's Black Guard, the elite protective force that the Head Council used to keep order amongst the different berserker groups.

Apparently, Stefen's superior intelligence was deemed useful enough to spare his life.

Ty slammed his fist on the table. "Damn it, Stefen! Can you shut the fuck up so that we can get the hell out of here?" Stefen looked startled before returning to his seat.

"It's okay," Wade said, putting a calming hand on Stefen's shoulder. He gave Ty a warning look. "We need to know as much as we can about our enemy and studying the group that had defeated them in the past will help."

Adam folded his arms. "Right, so what do we know?" When Stefen opened his mouth to answer, Adam held up a hand. "Someone else give the recap. We need to make sure we're all on the same page."

"The Bashar were created after the Blood War to hunt down and kill a deadly type of supe called the bloodborne," Erich said.

Ty rubbed his shoulder. "They were great fighters, masters of multiple fighting styles."

"This new supe is fast," Wade said. "I've never heard of anything faster than an Mti warrior's ability to shift. I couldn't keep up with him, even with the help of the trees."

Adam asked. "Do we know what kind of supes the Bashar were?" The room fell silent except for Stefen who was practically jumping out of his seat. Adam nodded to him.

"They are unlike any supernatural we have ever dealt with," he said, tapping on his tablet. "They are first mentioned in Julius Scorovan's journal from right after the Blood Era. Two thousand years ago, the end of the Blood War, brought about an era known as The Great Hunt, where followers of the demon, Sabien, were exterminated by the Bashar. The Bashar were greatly respected but also feared. They could detect that a person had supernatural powers and what those powers were. This is what allowed them to find the bloodborne, who looked human, when they weren't drinking blood, that is."

"Does that guy's journal mention anything about the bloodborne?" Adam asked.

Stefen shook his head. "Only that they were eradicated after the Blood War. After the last bloodborne was killed, the Bashar continued their mission and proceeded to slaughter every supe they came across, even the ones with no offensive capability, like the alara."

Erich's stomach clenched at the mention of alara, his mind immediately going to Sadie. Sadie who could be a victim of this psychotic supe. Sadie with her throat ripped out, her blood drained, her beautiful eyes staring at nothing. "So the Bashar are madmen."

"Unfortunately, so," Stefen said. "Once their initial mission was complete, they adapted and broadened their crusade against all supes. They slaughtered all supes with religious zeal. They believed that because their gift gave them the power to recognize a supe, even when glamoured, it was their duty to eradicate them. Their motto was 'See and Cleanse.'"

"They sound pleasant," Ty muttered.

Stefen shook his head, his face solemn. "They were not."

"So the Bashar were created to kill the bloodborne, but once their mission was complete, they killed other supes. We're no closer to figuring out what this new supe is. It could be anything," Brandt said.

Erich leaned back in his chair. "The bloodborne are a start. The name alone makes me think that this new supe is related somehow."

"Stefen, see what you can find out about the bloodborne," Adam said, standing to his feet. Stefen was already tapping on his iPad.

"Will do. I suspect that the Sardovian Archive of Antiquities will have something on them. There was an Intellect there by the name of Finnicus Doe who specialized in the Blood War— "

"Fine," Adam said. "Do what you need to do." As the rest of the men filed out of the room, Adam signaled for Erich to stay behind.

"How did it feel going out into the field?" he asked.

Erich shrugged. "It was good. I thought I would be rusty but I fell right into the swing of things."

Adam watched him, his blue eyes thoughtful. "How are things with the doc?"

Erich hesitated, a bit thrown at the change of subject. "Things are fine. I haven't touched her, if that's what you're asking."

"Wade came to me before the debrief. He's worried," Adam said.

Erich thought back to all of his recent encounters with Wade, trying to think of a time where he said or did the wrong thing. His mind came up empty.

"About what?"

"He said you're distracted by the doc. He's worried that you might be a liability out in the field." Adam raised his hand when Erich started to protest. "Don't worry, he said you were perfectly fine tonight, but he's still worried. We can't afford to have our minds elsewhere when we're on a job."

Erich chuckled. "I would think that all of you would be used to this by now. She's been here for how long? A year?"

Adam's eyes narrowed. "Used to what?"

"Being around an alara."

Adam was silent, as he looked at Erich in much the same way Wade had when he had mentioned his attraction to the alara. Adam finally shook his head.

"Being around an alara? What are you talking about?"

Erich swallowed hard. "I thought…I mean…You don't feel anything for Sadie?"

"Sure, I do. She's my employee, so I feel protective. She's a nice woman, smart, good at her job," Adam said with a shrug.

"Oh," Erich said, trying to process that new information. It wasn't easy under his brother's suspicious stare.

"When I first introduced you to her, you almost went nuclear," Adam prompted.

Erich's head snapped up. "No, it wasn't like that. I didn't feel any rage at all. In fact, I was totally at peace for the first time since I was a kid."

"So peaceful that you grabbed her," Adam said. He held up his hand to silence Erich's protest. "The fact of the matter is that something happened to you."

"I know," Erich said. "I thought it was an effect of being around an alara, but apparently not." His voice trailed off as he realized the implications. "So, it's just me."

"Tell me exactly what you feel," Adam ordered.

Erich's head was still spinning from the realization that what he was going through was not, in fact, a normal reaction to being in close proximity to an alara. It was something unique to him. Something was wrong with him. His skin felt overly hot as he recounted his past encounters with Sadie. It wasn't all bad. For a berserker to feel calm was an ideal state of being and extremely hard to achieve. But his lack of control toward her and fierce protectiveness was cause for concern. In the field, distractions could lead to his death. Or worse, the death of his team.

Adam listened intently, his arms folded across his chest and staring into the middle distance. After a few moments of silence, he straightened and looked at his brother. "I'm not going to lie, this worries me," he said. "But it's good that you told me everything. We can't fix it if we don't know about it."

Erich hesitated. "That's the thing, I don't want to fix it.

Sadie makes me feel fucking fantastic. I can't let you take that away."

"The mission always comes first, brother," Adam said, fixing him with a fierce glare. "You know that."

Erich's back stiffened. "Like I said, I can't let you take her away," he said.

The two brothers stared at each other, locked in a standoff that neither were willing to end first. To be honest, Erich understood where Adam was coming from. Feelings like this could derail the entire company. But deep down, he knew that separating him from Sadie was not going to end well. He would tear the building apart to get to her. Adam seemed to sense the same.

"Let's figure out what this is before we make any decisions," he said. "I'll have Stefen look into it. Maybe there's a way to deal with it that doesn't involve separating the two of you."

Erich nodded in relief. He relaxed hands that he hadn't realized were clenched. Adam grabbed his shoulder in a sign of affection.

"Don't worry, brother. We'll figure something out," he said.

Erich hoped so. He had a sneaking suspicion that if anyone tried to separate him from his woman, he'd tear their entire world apart.

CHAPTER 14

*S*adie tossed the tablet onto her desk with a sigh and rubbed her eyes. A quick glance at the clock told her that it was way past time to call it a day, but with the increase in bloodborne attacks and the delay's in the serum, she couldn't seem to find a good stopping point. To be honest, after yesterday's conversation with her sister, she wasn't sure she even wanted to go home. She hated the look of accusation in Lauren's eyes, but the worse part was knowing that her lies had hurt one of the most important people in her life. She had never been the type to hide from her problems, though, and sitting in her office was not going to help the situation.

With a sigh, she stood and grabbed her messenger bag. She turned and shrieked as she noticed someone standing in the doorway.

Erich held up his hands. "Sorry to scare you, doc."

Letting out a nervous laugh, Sadie swung her bag onto her shoulder. "It's okay. You just startled me." She didn't know if her rapid heart rate was due to the scare, or the cause as he lounged deliciously against the doorjamb.

"Well, let me make it up to you," Erich said. He smiled as she drew closer.

"Make it up to me?" she asked, turning off her office lights. "How?"

"Dinner," he said. "With the best chef in Triton City. Chef Georges."

Sadie frowned. "Isn't he in the cafeteria?"

Erich nodded.

"I eat lunch at the cafeteria every day," she said. "The food is good, and all, but I don't know if I'd call it the best in the city."

"So you've never eaten dinner here?"

Sadie shook her head.

"You're missing out. Chef Georges saves all of his good recipes for dinner."

"Why?"

"Less people, less of a hurry. Usually it's just us fighters here at night, so he tries to make things special for us," he said. Sadie flushed under the weight of his stare. She had planned on heating up a frozen lasagna for dinner. Not great, but it was edible.

"Maybe I should give it a try. What's on the menu for tonight?"

"What's today?"

"Tuesday."

"It's steak night," Erich said.

Sadie lifted an eyebrow. "You have the menu memorized?"

Erich shot her a curious glance. "Of course," he said. "Why wouldn't I? That's the first thing I researched when I came here."

Sadie chuckled. "Well, I *am* pretty hungry," she admitted. Erich's face brightened and he placed her hand on his arm like he was a gentleman escorting a lady.

"Then allow me to introduce you to the wonders of Odinshield's dining facility," he said, leading her down the hall.

When they walked into the cafeteria, Sadie was immediately bombarded by the most delicious smell. Her stomach growled as she looked around expectantly. After Erich's boasting, she half expected the place to have been transformed into a fine dining establishment, but it looked like the same cafeteria. Booths and tables were placed in tidy rows throughout most of the large room. To the right, stood the grab-and-go items. That was where she normally headed when she would come here for lunch. The refrigerated wall was now empty and waiting for the next day's wraps and fruit cups. There was no need for registers since all food was complimentary to Odinshield employees. Adam valued loyalty and he was smart enough to know that happy employees tended to be loyal employees.

Erich led her to the main grill. The head chef, Georges, was standing nearby, annotating something in a notebook. His head shot up when he heard them approach.

"Erich!" he bellowed. "My favorite customer!"

"I bet you say that to all the boys," Erich said. The chef shot his head back and gave a big laugh.

"That I do," he said. His eyes alighted onto Sadie. "You brought the doctor. What a nice surprise! What would you like, a turkey wrap?"

Sadie blinked in surprise as he recited her normal lunch back to her. She rarely spent any time in the cafeteria, and normally just grabbed her turkey wrap and salad and left. She had no idea he was keeping such close tabs on her. The chef laughed again.

"Don't look so surprised, my dear. I know what everyone likes. That's my job."

"I was telling her about your delicious steaks," Erich said. "She said she can't wait to try one."

Chef Georges looked at her in surprise. "I am honored," he said. "I'll find the best cut of meat for you, Sadie." Georges beamed at her before hustling behind the kitchen door.

"Get the best for me too," Erich yelled after him, but it was too late. He stared at the swinging door glumly.

Sadie squeezed his arm. "Don't worry, if your steak is bad, I'll share mine with you."

Erich looked down at her and grinned. "The last thing I would do is take something as delicious as Georges' steaks away from you. I want you to savor every bite."

"Wow, this food had better live up to its reputation," Sadie said.

"Don't worry. It will. Our first date should absolutely have the best food."

Sadie's stomach flipped. "Is this a date?" she asked.

"I'd like for it to be…if you'll have me," Erich said, smiling down at her.

Shyness suddenly overtook her and she looked away. A part of her wanted to affirmatively declare that, yes, she would indeed have him. With his looks, women must fall all over themselves just to get his attention. But one thing her childhood has taught her is that relationships are fickle, empty things. People tended to love those who they can use for their own needs. Still, a strong handsome man was asking her on a date and she wasn't against spending time with members of the opposite sex.

"Well," she said. "It depends on how good these steaks are."

Erich grinned. "Good. Then it's a date because Georges' cooking is the best I've ever had."

Consciously aware of the strange tingling in her stomach, Sadie shifted her bag onto her other shoulder.

"So, um, what do we do now?" she asked. Erich grabbed two sodas from the industrial refrigerator and motioned for her to follow him.

"I normally sit over here and read or watch the game," he said, gesturing to the TV on the wall. He placed their sodas on the table and invited her to sit. He slid into the booth opposite her. "But tonight I have a better view."

Sadie felt her cheeks warm as she smiled down at the table. Erich laughed softly.

"I'm sorry. I can't seem to stop overstepping when I'm around you," he said.

Sadie waved her hand dismissively. "No, it's okay. I mean, you're not overstepping." Erich looked relieved before dropping his gaze to the soda in his hand.

"So, since this is a date, I feel tradition dictates that we get to know each other," Erich said.

Sadie nodded. "Yes, that's usually what happens."

"Good, so we're in agreement. Tell me about yourself."

Sadie froze. For the first time she noticed that there were golden specs within the blue of his eyes. "Um…"

"Want me to go first?" Erich asked with a grin.

Sadie laughed and nodded. What was wrong with her? She was perfectly capable of telling a handsome man the basic details of her life, but for some reason, her mind drew a complete blank whenever she locked eyes with him.

Erich took a drink of his soda and leaned back. "Well, I have one brother, as you know. My mother lives in Cedar Creek now, but I grew up in Barstead."

"Was your father a berserker?" Sadie asked.

Erich shrugged. "I don't know. He died when I was a baby. Judging from some of my mother's stories, I would say yes. He got in a lot of bar fights but nothing too serious. I don't know for sure."

Sadie nodded. "The berserker gene has been known to

skip generations. If your father wasn't, your grandfather might have been."

"We'll never know. He died long before I was born," Erich said. "What about you? What are your parents like?"

Sadie was spared from answering by the arrival of their food. As soon as she smelled the aroma coming from her plate, her stomach growled. She must have been hungrier than she had thought because even the mention of her parents wasn't enough to kill her appetite.

They ate in companionable silence, both lost in the wonders of Georges' cooking. Erich hadn't been exaggerating when he said Georges was the best chef in town. The steak was cooked medium-well, but seemed to melt in her mouth. She popped the last piece into her mouth and sighed.

Sadie pushed her plate away. "That was amazing," she said.

"Told you," Erich said with a lopsided grin.

"I had no idea this was here. I could have been eating like a queen every night."

"And now you shall," Erich said. "I come down around 1800. You should join me."

Sadie could feel the heat growing on her cheeks as Erich watched her expectantly. He looked completely relaxed, like he hadn't just asked her out on a daily dinner date. Meanwhile, her heart was pounding so hard, she felt a little faint. Her fingers twisted around the paper napkin in her lap.

"Well, I normally eat dinner with Lauren, when she's not studying late or spending time with her boyfriend."

Erich's grin broadened. "Bring her along. The more the merrier."

That was unexpected. Maybe he wasn't asking her on a date, after all. "Oh," she said. "Yes, Lauren would love it."

"Me too," Erich said, raising his arm to signal to Georges. "As long as I'm with you, I'm happy."

Sadie blinked. Ignoring the pounding of her heart, she tried to focus on the conversation between Erich and the chef. He's happy as long as he's with her? So he *was* asking her on more dates. Her head swam as she tried to make sense of his words.

"Sadie?"

Sadie looked up to find two sets of eyes trained on her.

"You okay, doc?" Erich asked.

"Oh, yes, of course," she said, setting her shredded napkin on the table. The room grew silent as everyone stared at her. She raised her eyebrows in question.

Georges cleared his throat. "Would you like key lime pie or the chocolate cake for dessert?"

Pie or cake. Georges asked such a casual question like the most handsome man in the world hadn't just asked her out on, not just one date, but multiple dates. A standing invitation. Every day at six in the evening.

"Uh," Erich said. "Let's just do both."

Georges nodded, and with one last worried glance in her direction, he scurried off toward the kitchen.

Erich waved his hand in front of her face. "You okay, Sadie?" he asked, his face looking worried.

Sadie laughed and pressed her hands to her cheeks. "Yes, I'm fine. I don't know why I spaced out back there."

Erich raised an eyebrow and nodded. "Food coma. It's a real thing," he said. "When we were kids, Adam and I used to ride our bikes to town so that we could go to this all you can eat buffet. It was slamming! I'm talking about roast beef, ham, fried chicken...everything a boy would want."

Thankful for the change in subject, Sadie said, "I can imagine the look on your mother's face."

Erich shrugged. "It was just us. My mother never remarried, so she worked double-time to pay the bills."

That was a common theme amongst berserkers. Most of

them never get a chance to grow up with their fathers. Untrained berserkers tended to have short life spans.

Sadie shook her head and smiled. "I can imagine young Erich gleefully gorging on a buffet, but Adam? He's so serious. Did he frown the whole time?"

Erich threw his head back and laughed. "No, in fact, Adam wasn't always so serious. He was a normal kid until his berserker gene was turned on."

"What flipped it on?"

Erich's smile faded. He shook his head. "That's Adam's story to tell," he said.

Sadie held up her hand. "Oh, I'm sorry," she said. "I didn't know it was private."

"No, you're okay," Erich said. He reached across the table and took her hand. "It's just, that situation tends to be traumatic. It's not something we like to talk about."

Sadie dropped her gaze, watching as his hand, so capable of such death and destruction, gently held hers. Now that he mentioned it, none of the guys had ever discussed their transformation. Not even in passing.

"I don't mind telling you mine, though," Erich said

"You don't have to," Sadie said. "I shouldn't have brought it up."

"No, it's okay. I want you to know."

Sadie raised her gaze to meet his. He gave her a little smile like he was reassuring her that everything was okay.

"I was seventeen. I had grown a little rebellious ever since Adam had left for the protective force. I got into trouble every now and then, but nothing too serious."

Sadie tried to picture Erich as a teenager. He would have had the same sandy blond hair and bright blue eyes, of course, but at seventeen, he was probably just beginning to fill out.

"So, anyway, I was driving my mom's car out of town to

meet up with some friends when this guy cut me off," Erich ran his hand through his hair and sighed. "We went at it a little. Road rage. We were both acting stupidly. Weaving through traffic, shooting each other the finger. Eventually, the guy cut in front of me and clipped my bumper. I lost control and went crashing into the highway barrier."

"Were you okay?"

"Yeah, nothing was wrong with me physically but looking back? The rage was there. Not to berserker levels, but it was there."

His voice faltered. He leaned back and cleared his throat. Sadie squeezed his hand, urging him to go on.

"So I got out of my car, ready to beat the shit out of the guy. And the guy was pissed, too. He came at me and after that first punch, I lost it." Erich slipped his hands out of hers and pressed his palms on the table. "I took a punch to the chin and my switch got flipped. Any other time, I would have been fine. I would have kicked his ass and went about my day. But the fight combined with the road rage," Erich shook his head. "It was a perfect storm."

Georges arrived with their desserts. Erich looked relieved as he shoved his dinner plate to the side to make room.

"Chocolate cake for the gentleman, and key lime pie and cake for the lady," he announced as he set the dessert plates in front of them.

Erich dug in, the trauma of his transition seemingly forgotten. Sadie picked at the key lime pie, her heart wrenching for the teenage boy who was forced to experience the berserker rage before he was even able to experience a full life. She didn't have to ask what happened next. Due to his older brother, Erich would have been a known entity. Wolveshire would have been keeping a close eye on him and as soon as his rage came out, they would have swooped in and shipped him to be trained as an Ulfhednar.

Sadie hated to bring it up, but she had to know. "So, the other guy. Did you…"

"No, I didn't kill him. He did end up in the hospital, though," Erich sighed and ran his hand through his hair. "Luckily, one of my early punches knocked him behind his car. I ended up taking my rage out on his car instead. When I woke up, it was in pieces and even law enforcement was afraid to get near me. I remember being so confused because as far as I knew, I had gone from being pissed at that guy to feeling weak as a baby in a matter of seconds. My mother had to fill me in on what I had done."

Sadie reached across the table and took his hand. "That must have been a lot for a teenager to handle."

"Yeah, my mother called Adam. He and a recruiter from Wolveshire came down to take me back for training."

"And the guy in the hospital?"

"Wolveshire took care of him. Paid his bills and paid him to not press charges. I definitely got off easy."

Sadie squeezed his hand. "Thank you for sharing with me."

Erich smiled. "I want you to know everything. I don't want any secrets between us."

Sadie dropped her gaze, feeling uncomfortable with the intimacy between them. She had never felt that way before. She was close with her sister, of course, but she was protective of Lauren, always having to put on a brave front. The closest she had to a true friend was her foster mother. Even then, the relationship was still more parent/child, even to this day.

"Since you told me such a personal story, I feel like I should return the favor," she said, glancing up. He was staring at her, his eyes soft.

"You don't have to. I don't want you to do anything you're uncomfortable doing."

Sadie hesitated, considering. Politeness told her that she should return the share, and to be honest, she liked this new intimacy between them, but caution held her tongue. For whatever reason, Erich seemed to like spending time with her and she didn't want to ruin it by telling him about her past.

She would have to tell him eventually, but maybe not on their first date.

"Actually, I should probably be going," she said, gathering her bag. "Thank you for dinner."

Erich smiled. "My pleasure," he said, matching her steps as they headed toward the door. "I never did get an answer though."

Sadie froze, her bag dangling from her hand. "An answer?"

Erich turned back when he noticed that she had stopped walking. "Yeah, our dinner date. I come down every night at around six, so … Tomorrow is seafood night and his seafood surprise is amazing."

Sadie instantly felt her cheeks grow hot. "Sometimes I have plans with Lauren, but I'd love to meet you tomorrow?"

Erich's face broke into a goofy grin. "Great, it's a date. I'll pick you up at six."

Sadie laughed at the idea of Erich having to make the long trek down the hallway to pick her up. "I'll be ready."

CHAPTER 15

*E*rich racked the weights with a grunt and sat up. Breathing heavily, he rotated his right arm, trying to work out the stiffness. He was really regretting letting himself get out of shape while on the outside.

At the time, he had been happy to be rid of the daily workouts. In fact, during the first month of freedom, he had sat on his ass and gorged on carbs. But old habits die hard and he had eventually bought a gym membership so he could at least lift a couple of times week. Of course, not willing to live under someone else's rules, especially a human civilian's, Erich ended up buying the gym and turning it into a fighting gym. Profits doubled after the first month.

He still had a long way to go if he was going to get into fighting shape. He sighed. Fighting was in his blood, but he didn't know if he even wanted to go back to that life. The years living as a clueless civilian was actually kind of nice. On the few occasions where his blood lust had become unbearable, a few rounds in the octagon or between the thighs of a beautiful woman had calmed him down enough to be a normal functioning member of society. It was always there, though. The rage. A siren song drawing him toward the thrill of battle, the tangy smell of his victim's blood, and the thrill of victory. Just thinking about it made his heart beat faster.

He shook himself and grabbed his water bottle. He emptied it in a few gulps, hoping the water would both hydrate and calm him.

"I see you're finally doing something about that spare tire."

Erich counted to ten before looking up. "What do you want, Ty?"

Ty smirked as he leaned against a treadmill. "The boss is looking for you. He's been pinging your watch for the last 15 minutes. There's a letter from the Academy of Sardova."

Erich checked his watch and grimaced at the seven missed messages. The Academy was where the smartest people in the world studied Sardovian history, and other things that went way above Erich's head. He stood and wiped down the bench. "What does a letter from Sardova have to do with me?"

"Probably a detailed thesis on how much of a dumbass you are for losing it in a street fight."

Erich froze, the familiar icy tingle running down his spine. He took a deep breath, his hands involuntarily closing into fists.

Ty watched him with interest. "You good?"

Erich took a couple of breaths, staring at the far wall until his heart rate returned to a normal level. Between Ty and Sadie, he was going to have a damn meltdown and kill everyone in the building.

"I almost had you," Ty said, a little too gleefully. "Your eyes did change, though. For a split second."

"Shut up," Erich said, pushing past him. Ty followed him into the hall.

"Maybe I should go get the doc. She seemed to set you off —" he let out a grunt as his body slammed into the wall.

"You don't lay a finger on her, understand?" Erich seethed through gritted teeth.

Ty's characteristic smirk was gone. "That triggered it," he said. "What is it about her that makes you go nuclear?"

Erich abruptly released him. "You were testing me." It was more a statement of fact than a question.

"You're damn right I was. Adam told me about this thing between you and the doc."

Erich ran his hand through his sweat-dampened hair. Ever since that day in the clinic, he hadn't been able to keep his mind off of her. He woke with Sadie on his mind and she was the last thing he thought about before he went to sleep. It was downright pathetic. He'd been with plenty of women, but here he was mooning over a woman who he'd barely even touched.

No matter what it was, he wasn't about to spill his guts to Ty of all people. "Can anyone keep a secret around here? I told him that in confidence."

Ty shook his head. "Not with something like this. This affects all of us. This connection you feel is making you unstable and unpredictable. That's not exactly an ideal state of being for people like us."

"Whatever," Erich said as he bent to retrieve the water bottle and towel he had dropped. "One thing I know is that I'm not talking about it with you. Where's Adam?"

"Penthouse conference room."

As Ty punched the button to call the elevator, Erich had the sudden need to be alone. Thirty seconds in a metal box with the most annoying asshole on the planet was not what he needed at that moment.

"I'm taking the stairs," he announced before pivoting toward the stairwell.

"Don't be late," Ty yelled after him.

Erich took the steps three at a time, his long legs relishing the workout. By the time he reached the top floor, his breathing was labored and he was seeing spots in front of his eyes. Totally worth it though because for those few precious minutes, he had forgotten about blood-soaked alleyways and sexy doctors. Clutching the bottled water he had taken from the gym fridge, he sat on the top step to catch his breath. There was no way he was rolling up in there, red-faced and panting like a dog.

Properly composed, he pressed his watch in front of the sensor and pushed through the heavy exit door into Adam's plush penthouse suite. He pivoted to the right and strode toward Adam's office, which took up half of the floor. His secretary, Julie, was at her desk and gave him a quick wave.

"You're late," she said. Erich flashed his most charming smile but she just rolled her eyes and looked back at her computer. Damn, he must be getting rusty. He was usually pretty good with the ladies. He'll never get the doc at this rate.

All thoughts of his love life screeched to a halt as he pushed through the door. He froze as twelve sets of eyes turned to look at him.

"Am I late?" he asked. Adam waved him in.

"Sit down. Stefen was just about to tell us what he learned from his contact at the Sardovian Academy."

"Keep it short," Ty muttered. Stefen ignored him.

"The Academy has been keeping records of berserker history ever since Wolveshire was founded," he said, handing Adam a thick report with the Sardovian Academy's seal on the cover. "Because our founder was the first cousin of the

Air Elemental, the intellects at the Academy were very interested in the relationship between berserkers and elementals."

"What did they find out?" Adam asked.

"Not much, I'm afraid," Stefen said. "The elemental power still flows to a woman of Sardovian blood upon the previous elemental's death without respect to genetic history. It's totally random. There doesn't seem to be any connection to berserker blood."

Ty sighed loudly. "What does this have to do with Erich's problem?"

"I'm getting to that," Stefen snapped. "One cannot understand the present without knowing their history."

"Ty, shut the hell up," Adam said. "Stefen, skip ahead to what's immediately relevant."

Stefen frowned as he gathered his thoughts. "Five hundred years ago, a berserker by the name of Bo Eidsson became so obsessed with his neighbor's new wife, there was no consoling him. The enforcement services at the time did everything they could to keep them apart but there was no stopping him. Fines, imprisonment, banishment. Nothing worked. Even Wolveshire couldn't control him. Eventually, he murdered the woman's husband and ran off with her."

"So what happened to him?" Erich asked.

Stefen shrugged. "No one knows. He was never heard from again. After that, the Academy intellects worked with the Head Council to figure out what happened. Turns out, that was not the first time a berserker had gone obsessive, it was just the most tragic."

The room grew quiet. Putting himself in the man's situation made Erich uncomfortable. If Sadie was already married, getting rid of her husband seemed like a logical solution. The fact that Erich couldn't find fault with that logic worried him.

"There's a reason why berserkers tend to live solitary

lives. There's a one in a million chance of meeting your true life partner. She's called a boratai," Stefen said. "A boratai is someone, usually a woman, who connects with both man and his beast. Once he meets his lifemate, the berserker will be permanently and catastrophically attached to her."

"Mate? What am I? A damn shifter?" Erich asked, trying to lighten the mood.

Ty nodded. "Yep. Next thing you know, you'll be rutting like an animal and howling at the moon."

Brandt folded his arms across his chest, his pale eyes haunted. "I don't know, Adam. This sounds made up. Maybe this feeling is just normal love. Why haven't we heard about this before now?"

"Because berserkers are usually dead or in jail by the time they reach our age." Stefen said.

"Or living in their frozen castle up north," Ty said. "The closest women to Wolveshire are thirty miles away. Perfect distance for a quick roll in the hay before leaving town."

"Still," Brandt said. "There have been marriages in our past. Stefen, your father is still alive, did he go through this?"

Stefen shrugged. "I don't know. I can ask. As far as I could tell, my parents had a normal marriage, like every other civilian."

"I don't like this," Brandt said, dropping his gaze to the table. "I don't like the idea of being catastrophically attached to someone." Erich didn't have to think very hard to know why. There was no such thing as secrets around here, and he had heard about Brandt's past when he first returned to Odinshield. Death camps. Cage fights. It wasn't pretty. Someone who grew up in that environment was understandably uncomfortable with not having control.

Adam crossed his arms. "We don't know how common this is. I, for one, have never heard of it. There's a good chance that this will not happen to anyone else." Brandt didn't respond, his gaze fixed on the table.

Adam tossed the paper onto his desk. "All that aside, there are security implications to this. We've seen how Erich reacts to someone who just mentions touching Sadie. All an enemy would have to do is threaten our boratai to control us. They would be a weakness."

"Couldn't that be said for all of us? If our enemies take one of us, wouldn't we do what it takes to get him back?" Wade asked.

"This is different," Erich said, rubbing at a strange throbbing sensation in his chest. "With Sadie, I'll go through any one of you to protect her. Even Adam. I have a feeling I'll kill anyone who stands between us."

The room grew silent. Everyone in their own thoughts.

"So what does that mean?" Ty asked. "We shut ourselves off from the world? Go back north? Go into isolation?"

"We hang tight and go about our business, as usual," Adam said. He hesitated before adding, "I have to tell the council about this. They need to know about this potential weakness."

Ty huffed. "Great. Let's just leave all of this up to a bunch of out of touch old farts."

"They'll want to rehabilitate him," Brandt said, his voice low. "They won't allow Erich to be a weak link."

"There's no amount of rehabilitation that can change what I'm feeling. They can try, but they won't succeed," Erich said.

Brandt looked at him with haunted eyes. "Don't be so sure," he said.

"You're not going anywhere," Adam said. "I'm not handing you over to be drugged and rehabilitated."

Stefen spoke up. "You do know that you're talking about insubordination. The Head Council won't take that kindly."

"They will have to leave their frozen castle to do anything about it," Adam said. "But I won't endanger the rest of you. This is my fight. If you disagree, I'll step down and Wade will take over."

"That'll be hard to do considering I'll be standing with you," Wade said. "We stand together. When one of our own is threatened, we close ranks."

Erich swallowed the lump in his throat. "I can't ask that of you. If the Head Council wants me to go north, I'll go. I won't be putting anyone else in danger for my own bullshit." Erich gestured toward Brandt. "Especially those of you who don't even know me."

"No," Brandt said. "Wade is right. From the sound of it, this could have happened to any of us. We need to get ahead of this before the standard operating procedure becomes shipping us to Wolveshire for Tier 3 rehabilitation."

"Exactly," Adam said. "Most of us know what happens when higher-ups try to control our emotions. I won't let that happen again."

"The serum," Erich said. "You have Sadie working on a new formula to control our rage. I can take it to mellow me out a bit."

Adam shook his head. "We're not any closer to targeting specific emotions. If you take the prototype that we have now, you'll lose all emotion, even the good ones. Is that what you really want? To feel nothing for Sadie? To feel nothing at all?"

Just the thought of not being around Sadie made him antsy. He resisted the urge to get up and pace around the room. Instead he leaned his elbows on the table and rested his head on his hands. He didn't want to lose the feeling he had for Sadie, but if he took the serum, he wouldn't feel any loss. He wouldn't care one way or the other.

Honey brown hair. Deep rich eyes. A smile more beautiful than any sunrise he'd ever seen.

His Sadie.

Could he exist in this world without her belonging to him? Even with the effects of the serum, he suspected that he would still feel a sense of loss. Like half of his body was missing.

Still, he couldn't bring the wrath of the Head Council down on his brothers. The Ulfhednar clan was large and deadly. Unlike the undisciplined scrubs of the Frelshednar, Ulfhednar boys with the berserker gene trained from puberty in the art of fighting and the skill of controlling their rage. The men of Odinshield were tough fighters, but they wouldn't stand a chance against the might of Wolveshire.

Erich looked around the room at the men who were as close as family to him. If he defied the Head Council, he would be responsible for all of their deaths.

"I think it would be best if—"

"No," Adam said.

Erich frowned. "It's my choice, Adam. Taking the serum would be better for all of us."

Adam leaned down and got in his face. "That's where you're wrong, brother. I'm the chieftain, it's my serum, therefore it's my decision. I know what it's like being on that stuff. This serum is not for you."

"He's right," Wade said. "You don't know what it's like. If you take the serum, we'd lose you one way or the other."

Erich couldn't contain himself and started pacing the room. "Okay, fine. I don't take the serum. Then what?"

Adam sighed. "Like I said earlier. We wait and see what the Head Council has to say."

Erich stopped by the window and stared at the sparkling lights of Triton City. All of those people who are just going about their lives. Waking up, going to work, coming home, maybe fucking their wives, and then going to bed. Only to do the same thing the next day. Meanwhile, he felt like he had his head on the chopping block. What would Sadie think about going up north if the council demanded it of them. They had just met and he wasn't even sure how she felt about him. Would she go? Would she even want to have anything to do with him once she found out about this whole boratai business?

"Okay," Erich said, turning back to the group. "But let's all agree that Sadie doesn't hear a word about this until we know for sure what's going on. I don't want her thinking that I'm an obsessed berserker or something."

"But isn't that the truth?" Ty asked.

Erich hesitated. If the tables were turned and Sadie was the one fated to be with him, he would find it flattering. In fact, he would jump at the idea of being with her.

Then again, that could be the boratai/mating thing talking.

The fact of the matter was that he couldn't fathom not being drawn to her. As a result, his opinion on the matter was obviously skewed.

Adam saved him from answering. "She doesn't need to know, yet. As a matter of fact, no one outside of the brotherhood needs to know. This is considered classified." He turned to his brother. "I would order you to stay away from her, but I know that's not going to do any good."

Erich nodded. It was obvious that asking him to not talk to Sadie was like asking him to stop breathing. Even if he tried, his body would eventually find a way.

After some last-minute discussions that Erich barely paid attention to, the men filed out of the conference room. Erich avoided all attempts at conversation. Now that he was on Wolveshire's radar, he needed to be alone to think.

As he let himself into his room, he tossed his water bottle

onto his bed. The shower was calling him, but first he needed to get his affairs in order. If he was recalled up north, he'd have to make sure Nia had everything she needed to run the gym. Judging from what he knew about Tier 3 rehabilitation, he probably needed to sign the gym over to her. There was a very real possibility that he wouldn't come back.

A soft knock interrupted his thoughts. He opened the door to find Sadie, her face flushed in such a way that made him consciously aware of how close his bed was to the door. Her eyes glittered with excitement and her soft lips were slightly parted. Erich blinked as a wave of erotic dizziness washed over him.

"Sadie…what…?"

Sadie silenced him with a hand on his arm that burned straight through his skin. "Erich, I'm sorry to drop by unexpectedly, but I need you."

CHAPTER 16

Sadie suppressed a laugh as Erich shifted his massive weight on the tiny stool. Jamison's lab had state-of-the-art equipment, but provided little when it came to personal comfort.

The man in question was now bent over a brown clipboard, slowly annotating his findings with the precise methodology of a man with nowhere to go.

Sadie leaned against a counter. "So, where have you been?"

Jamison straightened but didn't look away from his clipboard. "I had other engagements," he said. He moved to a cluttered desk and picked up his tablet.

"Business or personal?" Sadie asked, moving with him. Jamison didn't answer. Typical. While the guy was a bonafide genius, his social skills were seriously lacking. Adam insisted on working with him because he got results, but he wasn't the one who had to deal with the prickly scientist on a regular basis. Fortunately, this wasn't Sadie's first experience with this kind of personality. She'd helped raise a teenage girl, after all.

"Jamison?" He didn't respond, instead continuing to read something on his tablet.

Sadie snatched the device out of Jamison's hands. That got his attention. He made an attempt to grab it back, but Sadie was too fast.

"Listen, Jamison. Odinshield pays you a lot of money and they expect results," she snapped. She gestured toward the lab equipment. "All of this belongs to Odinshield. So unless you had a personal emergency, Adam wants all of your working hours figuring out this serum."

Jamison's face flushed. "Who are you to tell me what to do?" He snatched the tablet back and glared at her. "I've been doing this since you've been in diapers. Sit down, girl. I'll get to you when I'm done."

Sadie's back straightened. "First, you can address me as Dr. Carmichael. Second, I'm the link between you and the man who is paying you.

"You have no idea what I'm dealing with," he seethed, standing at his full height so that he could look down at her.

"Then tell me? Maybe we can help," Sadie said.

"This is above your level of comprehension, *Dr. Carmichael*," he said, spitting out her name like it was a curse. "And if you ever touch my stuff again—"

He clamped his mouth shut, his eyes bulging as he focused above her head. Sadie initially thought he was having a seizure before she felt an electric presence behind her. She spun around. Erich was standing there, arms folded and eyes narrowed.

"What will you do if Dr. Carmichael touches your stuff?" he asked, his voice calm.

"I...I just meant..." Jamison's voice trailed off. As Erich let the silence hang for a minute, Jamison's face grew more red. Sadie could feel her own cheeks grow warm as the tension in the room grew. She placed her hand on Erich's arm and gave it a squeeze.

Erich glanced at her and then back to Jamison. "Sadie asked you a question," he said. "Answer her."

Jamison wetted his lips nervously. "My absence was due to a personal matter," he said.

"Are you alright? Can Odinshield help?"

"No," Jamison said, shaking his head. "I dealt with it. It's fine."

There wasn't much to say after that. The last thing she wanted to do was pry into his personal life. She gave Erich a small smile of thanks. He winked at her and strolled back to his tiny stool.

Jamison acted like a normal human being after that, answering all of her questions quickly and without attitude. Maybe she should bring Erich to every meeting with him.

Still, she breathed a sigh of relief as she gathered her bag to leave. While Jamison's work was interesting, she hated dealing with the man. Even when he was on his best behavior, he was still annoying.

"How did you find this guy, anyway?" Erich asked as he held the door open for her. Sadie smiled her thanks as she stepped through the doorway.

"Adam found him," she said. "Jamison is the top scientist in the field of supernatural genetics."

Erich snorted. "Top scientist in the field, or only scientist in the field?"

"Well," Sadie said. "A bit of both, I guess. There aren't many who believe supernaturals even exist."

Erich gave her a knowing look as if to say "no shit". "There're *no* scientists that believe we exist. Well, besides this guy, of course. And that's how it should be."

"That's what I don't understand. I asked Adam, but he's pretty tight-lipped about it."

"About what?"

Two ladies approached them from the opposite direction, talking excitedly over the contents of a file one of them was carrying. Sadie waited until the steady clicking of their heels faded before answering.

"The secrecy. Shifters, witches, berserkers," she waved her hand in his direction. "People like you could take over every realm in Tesselyn and the rest of us wouldn't be able to do a thing about it."

Erich arched his eyebrow. "Rest of us? As an alara, you're supernatural too."

Sadie nudged him with her elbow. "You know what I mean."

"You're right. Some do try to take control, but supes tend to work behind the scenes. Instead of being king, they manipulate the king to get what they want."

"That's what I mean," she said. "Why the secrecy? From what I've read, supernaturals used to be normal members of society. Even respected. There was an alara at every court and elementals traveled from realm to realm ensuring nature remained in balance."

"About a thousand years ago, supes were hunted and killed by a group called The Bashar," Erich said.

Sadie gasped. "What? Why?"

"They felt it was their duty. They had the power to detect the supernatural gene even if the person was trying to pass as human. Our founder encountered one while he was escorting some elementals. That was part of the reason he developed the Ulfhednar. Supes needed protection, especially the vulnerable ones, like alara."

Sadie stared straight ahead as they walked down the long corridor. The idea of being hunted just because of who you were was eerily familiar. Her heart went out to all of those supes who were killed. Were her ancestors among them?

"That's terrible! If they could detect the supernatural gene, then that means they were supernatural themselves. Why did they deserve to live, and not everyone else?"

Erich shrugged. "They were a crazy cult. Why do groups like that do anything they do?"

Sadie rubbed the small knot on her inner arm. Why indeed? Why did the Children of Light worship her blood and no one else's? Why did her parents let their own daughter be used in such a way? She shuddered.

"You okay?" Erich asked. She gave him a shaky smile.

"Yes, just a little chilly."

He didn't look convinced but didn't seem to want to push the issue. She sighed in relief. They hadn't known each other for long, but she liked having him around. She dreaded having to tell him about her past. That was when most men grew distant and ended up disappearing off the face of the planet. She learned early in her dating life to never reveal the truth about her childhood and the Children of Light, but as she looked up at Erich's handsome face, she wanted him to be different. If she was going to let him into her life, even as a friend, she was going to have to tell him the truth about who she used to be and what she used to do.

"Come here," he said, putting an arm around her shoulder and pulling her close. "I'm always warm. I'll heat you up."

He wasn't lying. As he tucked her into his side, his body heat radiated off of him in waves. She sighed and settled into him as they walked toward the front of the building.

As soon as they left the building, they had to break apart as the heat of the sun made close contact unbearable.

"Thank you," Sadie said. "You really are a furnace."

"You know," Erich said, leaning in as if he was about to tell her a secret. "I'm a little psychic as well."

He looked downright giddy as he tried to lift the mood.

Sadie raised an eyebrow. "Are you? Adam never mentioned that."

Erich nodded, the sun highlighting the golden streaks in his hair. "It's true. We don't talk about it, but every berserker has a bit of witch in him. It's in our blood."

"Okay," Sadie said, suppressing a laugh. "What is your power?"

Erich looked offended. "I'm a little psychic. Weren't you paying attention?"

Despite her efforts, Sadie laughed. Erich's lip twitched, but he maintained a serious face.

"I'm telling you my deepest secrets, here. How can you laugh?"

Sadie wiped her eyes. "I'm sorry. Yes, I remember now that you said you were a little psychic. Please accept my deepest apology."

Erich looked away and sniffed. "Apology accepted, but I'm not sure I want to tell your future now."

Sadie grabbed his arm and pulled him toward her. "No, please. I must know what my future holds."

Erich quickly turned back to her with a goofy smile. "Okay," he said. Sadie giggled, but luckily he ignored it. "Give me your hand."

When she held up her right hand, he pushed it away. "No, woman. Your left, I can only read left palms."

She offered her left hand, palm up. He gently took her hand in his and stepped closer. Sadie's heart sped as she looked into his bright blue eyes. He gave a small smile before looking down at her palm. Released from his spell, she drew a deep shuddering breath, the spicy scent of his aftershave doing crazy things to her mind.

"Don't worry," Erich said looking up with a smile. "From what I can tell, it's a good future."

Sadie had never considered herself to be petite or dainty,

but seeing her hand engulfed by Erich's made her relax in a way she'd never experienced before. After years of having to be strong against the world, it felt good to be the one that was protected and sheltered. She knew this whole arrangement was temporary, but she could get used to having her own personal berserker to protect her. Especially one as attractive as Erich.

As he traced the lines of her palm with his finger, she felt as if he was touching her entire body. She shuddered.

"You still cold?" Erich asked.

"No," Sadie said with a giggle. When did she start giggling? She'd never giggled in her life. Spending her childhood with the Children of Light, watching over her sister while in foster care, and then working her way through med school didn't leave many opportunities for such things. One day with this man and she was giggling like a schoolgirl. "I mean...what's my future?"

Erich grinned at her and looked back at her palm. His eyes lit up. "You have a bright future!"

"I do?"

"Yes," he said. "Absolutely. You don't realize it yet, but you've already met the man of your dreams."

"I have?"

"Yes!"

"Who is he?" Sadie asked. She laughed as Erich squinted at her palm in concentration.

"I can't see his name, but I can tell he's very handsome and brave."

"What else?"

Erich paused his blue eyes rising to meet hers. "He will do anything to make you happy. He'll treat you like a queen," he said, his voice soft.

The air suddenly grew warm as they gazed at each other. She seemed to have forgotten how to breath as he held her in place with just a soft touch of his hand and the gentle look in his eyes.

"Anything else?" she whispered. Erich pulled her hand toward him, drawing her closer until her chest barely touched his.

"He will be utterly devoted to you," Erich whispered, leaning down so that his mouth hovered just above hers. She didn't know if it was his soap or his aftershave, but he smelled amazing. He smelled like spice and comfort and danger. She leaned in but resisted the urge to completely close the small gap between them. To do so would take their friendship to a different level and she didn't know if she was ready for that.

She had had a couple of boyfriends while in college, but those relationships paled in comparison to what she was feeling at this very moment. She suspected that if she crossed this boundary, she would be inextricably bound to this powerful whirlwind of a man.

At that moment, she couldn't think of anything she'd rather be.

Erich didn't move, as if he was waiting for her to take the next step. She swayed, her eyes dropping to his mouth. He waited. Patiently. All she had to do was raise on her toes, just a little. Just an inch or two.

He jerked back and lifted his head to scan the parking lot. Without a word, he spun around and pulled Sadie behind him, holding her in place with one arm. Gripping his bicep, she peered around his broad shoulders. It was then that Sadie noticed the tall man walking toward them. The man was slender with shimmering golden tattoos that seemed to dance across his deep brown skin. He walked with a smooth gate as if he was floating along the ground. The tail of his jacket fluttered dramatically behind him, despite the lack of wind.

Erich relaxed slightly but kept his eye on the man. Unfazed, the man walked toward them.

"Relax, berserker," the man said, his accent thick and melodious. "I'm just passing through."

Erich didn't respond but watched him as he passed by. Once he was out of reach, Erich took her hand. "Fae," he said. "Come on, let's get out of here."

Grabbing her hand, he led her through the parking lot. As she climbed into the black SUV, she peeked at her bodyguard. Gone was the boyish suitor, cracking jokes about being a psychic. Erich had transformed back into the serious brooding berserker that was on a mission. It was night and day, like he had two personalities.

And she loved them both.

Love? No, that's silly. Love was definitely not on the table. Especially with her parents searching for her and a crazy supernatural monster hunting her down. She would definitely be a liability to any man crazy enough to attach himself to her.

But she couldn't deny that she was attracted to him. From the first moment she met him, she knew there was something special about him. And to be honest, with her past, if she wanted to feel safe, having a berserker in her life was the way to do it. Her mind flashed back to the feel of his arm, as he put his body between her and the potential threat. The way his bicep rippled under her hand as he held her in place. The way his broad back blocked any potential danger headed their way. She pitied any being that was on the wrong end of that much power.

Yet, she knew deep down, that she could diffuse that power with the slightest push of her finger. That all of that rage would never be turned against her.

As he wove through the Triton City rush hour traffic, she studied his profile. He kept his dirty blonde hair a little longer than most protective force types. It looked soft, like he didn't bother with gels or creams, and allowed the front to slightly curl over his forehead. His blue eyes were framed by a set of lashes whose thickness would make any woman envious. A strong patriarchal nose led to a set of full, kissable lips. The contrast between his angelic face and the death and destruction that can be caused by his own hand was jarring.

Sadie's gaze focused on his lips. Berserkers were known for their sexual exploits. How does berserker rage manifest itself in the bedroom? What happens when his self-control breaks? Will his eyes flash gold while making love?

Erich glanced over, catching her eye. She quickly looked away, blushing at being caught staring.

"You okay?" he asked.

"Yeah," she said, trying to keep her voice level. Going from ogling a handsome man to mundane conversation was a bit jarring. "I've never seen a Fae before."

Erich flipped on his signal as he turned into the main road. "You probably have. They usually glamour their appearance."

"Did you think he was going to hurt us? You didn't seem to trust him."

Erich shrugged. "There are few supernaturals that I trust. I've seen what they do. They rarely consider lives outside of their own kind to be important."

The silence stretched between them as Sadie's thoughts went back to that moment before the Fae man had interrupted them. That moment when he had been about to kiss her. If she had leaned in, raised on her toes just a little, and closed the gap between them, what would this drive home be like? Would that kiss be enough to propel them into a relationship? Or would it have been one of those things that they'd laugh about later. She watched Erich as he maneuvered through traffic, his eyes distant as if in thought.

A part of her regretted not accepting his invitation, but deep down, she knew it was for the best. As attractive as Erich was, she had baggage. No sane man would want to date a woman who was raising her kid sister and running from a cult. Sadie sighed and turned her attention to the road. The Odinshield headquarters building drew closer. It was probably best that the mysterious Fae man had interrupted them. There was only one person she could count on, and that was herself. Not just for her own life, but for Lauren's as well.

CHAPTER 17

*E*rich quickly jogged up the stairs to his second-floor apartment. Putting the key in the lock, he opened the door and paused, listening for movement. He didn't know what he expected, but he hoped the place was empty. At some point, he was going to have to tell his best friend that he probably wasn't coming back. That would, of course, open up all kinds of questions about where he was living and why. Eventually, it would come around to who he was. What he was. It was better to just avoid the whole conversation altogether.

The living room was empty and tidier than normal. Nia must have just left. There was a benefit to living with a neat freak. Nia was fine when she was home, but her area had to be absolutely spotless before she felt comfortable leaving. Something about being embarrassed if she died while she was out. She didn't want the people packing up her stuff to think she was messy. Erich sighed. Pretty morbid, if you asked him.

He had come for a reason, so might as well get started.

Erich went into his bedroom and pulled out his suitcase and his other duffel bag from his closet. Mentally kicking himself for not bringing more boxes, he shoved the rest of his clothes into the duffel bag. It's funny. Before he left Odinshield for the civilian life, he had been living a sparse life. Most of his possessions could fit into a large backpack.

After seven years as a civilian, he almost felt like a normal person. His closet still consisted of his basic uniform of jeans and black T-shirts, but it at least had some blue ones now. Don't even start on the books. Both he and his brother had always been avid readers, but once he escaped the nightly grind of blood and death, his reading habits exploded. Most of the books on the shelves lining the entire living room wall were his. He'd have to come back for them, which meant he'd have to run the risk of seeing his Nia again.

He straightened and looked around his bedroom. How much longer could he keep lying to one of his best friends? Living a double life was simple when he had first started, but even then, it had always felt off. Wrong. Now, with him back into the grind, there was no way he'd be able to keep both sides of his life a secret. He was either going to have to tell Nia the truth, or disappear from her life. The problem was that he didn't know which would hurt her less.

"There you are," a female voice said. Erich turned in surprise, his hand instinctively reaching for his knife.

Nia stood directly behind him, only a couple of feet of distance between them. How had she snuck up on him? His life was so crazy, he was losing his edge. Not a good thing if he was about to go back to fighting the dregs of supernatural society.

Nia held up her hands in an apologetic gesture. "Sorry for scaring you," she said, taking a seat on his bed. For the millionth time, he wondered why he wasn't attracted to her.

He obviously wasn't blind. The woman was beautiful and had the soft caring personality that every sane man yearned for, but it was like a brick wall stood between his eyes and his libido.

She was dressed for work, her slim-fit black slacks and form-fitting blouse perfectly accentuated her curves. She stared at him, her almond-shaped brown eyes and sharp jaw accentuated by a severe ponytail that ended in a large afro puff. His fingers itched to feel its softness, but he held back. Nia had made it clear from day one that touching her hair was tantamount to a crime.

Erich chuckled. "I wasn't scared."

"Sure," Nia said with a smirk. "Anyway, where have you been?"

Erich hesitated. He didn't know if he was ready for the truth to come out, but he hadn't had a chance to come up with a believable lie.

"I'm staying with my brother." That was the truth. He silently begged for her not to dig deeper.

Nia frowned. "You have a brother?"

Erich mentally cursed. When he was living as a civilian, he was trying so hard to forget his past that he had revealed very little about himself. His lies were coming back to bite him.

"Yes, I do," he said.

"Where does he live?"

"Right outside of town," Erich said. He cringed at Nia's gasp.

"You've had a brother here this whole time and didn't mention him? Did you have a fight or something? Why haven't I met him?"

Erich stuffed the rest of his clothes in his suitcase and grabbed his duffel bag. "Listen, Nia. I don't have time to go into all the details. I'm just here to grab a few things and head back."

Nia followed him into the living room. "Just like that? After all of our years as friends, you're just going to pack up and leave to live with some long-lost brother? Were you going to even say goodbye?"

"Of course I was."

"Oh yeah? When?"

This was the moment Erich was dreading. When Nia had her mind set on something, she was like a hungry dog with a bone. Knowing she wouldn't let it go until she was satisfied, he set his bag down and headed into the kitchen. Grabbing a soda from the refrigerator, he leaned against the counter.

"Okay, Nia. Here's the situation. My brother, Adam, and I used to work together doing personal security for a company called Odinshield Protection Agency."

Nia nodded. "I believe it. You're huge and I've seen you in the octagon."

"We got along fine, but I just got tired of the security thing. I wanted to branch out and do something else, you know?"

Nia waited for more explanation. When none was forthcoming, she raised an eyebrow. "Okay, so why the secrecy? Why am I just now hearing about your brother?"

Erich shrugged as he took a gulp of the soda. To be honest, outside of the guys at Odinshield, Nia was the only person he felt comfortable enough to call a friend. Why had he withheld that part of his life from her? It would have been completely normal for him to have an older brother nearby, but withholding that information for so long made it weird.

Nia watched him, her eyebrows raised like she was daring him to lie to her again.

Erich sighed and put his can down. "I love my brother,

but I wanted out of the business. I guess I took it a little too far by completely writing him out of my life."

Nia's eyes softened. "So, what made you go back?"

Erich shrugged. "I don't know, it was time, I guess."

"It didn't have anything to do with you coming home bloody?"

Erich's breath rushed out of his body as if someone had punched him in the stomach. "What?"

Nia pulled out her phone and tapped on the screen. "I saved the video," she said, scrolling through her files. Erich closed his eyes and cursed. The video feed. Of course. About a year ago, Nia had made him install one of those hidden security cameras right outside the door. It recorded a short video every time it sensed motion. He hadn't given it a second thought because on a personal level, he wished someone would be foolish enough to break in while he was home. But Nia was a human, a female one at that, and more fragile.

Well, she didn't look fragile at that moment. She looked like a damn gladiator as she held her phone in front of his face. He watched the video of himself stagger up to the door and fumble for his keys. He looked worse than he remembered. The entire front of his shirt was caked in blood. He winced at the memory.

"Oh, that's not all," she said, tapping on her phone some more before holding it back up. The video showed Wade and Tyrell walking to the door. They spoke to each other and then knocked on the door.

"And I have the video of you leaving," Nia said, tapping on her phone again. Erich held up his hand.

"I don't need to see the video," he said. "I was there."

"No shit," Nia said, setting her phone down. She leaned against the counter and crossed her arms. "Explain. And don't try to lie to me either."

Erich sighed and rubbed the back of his head. He hated lying to her, but the true mission of Odinshield was secret for a reason. His true nature was kept secret for a reason.

Nia crossed the kitchen and placed her hand on his arm. "Whatever it is, I will not judge you. You can trust me."

With her eyes soft with concern like that, Erich was almost tempted to tell her everything. They had been room-mates for over a year. He trusted Nia with his life. Besides, it would be nice to be able to confide in a friend about the fucked up situation he was in.

But telling her who he truly was would mean he would have to explain why he was in Triton in the first place. He would have to reveal the true nature of a berserker and why the Ulfhednar had decided to control the rage. Like most humans, she wasn't ready to learn about the never-ending fight against the supernaturals that refused to let the rest of the world live their lives in peace. He wasn't ready for her to know his true nature.

"That night, I got jumped." When Nia's eyes widened in concerned, he rushed on. "But I'm fine. They just got in a couple of lucky shots."

"They? How many were there?"

"Five."

"Five? You're lucky to be alive! Then again, you're a badass yourself, so I should probably ask how the five guys are doing." Nia said, with a laugh.

Erich plastered a smile on his face. His laugh sounded forced and hollow. "Yeah...." He said, his voice fading into an uncomfortable silence between them.

Nia waved her hand in a 'go on' motion. "Okay, you're obviously fine, so why are you moving out? Who were those two guys?"

"I used to work with them at Odinshield."

"And they just happened to show up the day you were jumped? Did you call them for help or something."

Erich dumped the rest of his soda in the sink and headed into the living room. "Come on, Nia. What's with all these questions?"

"I'm sorry if I'm concerned about my best friend showing up bloody and then disappearing with some guys for almost a week."

When she put it that way, it did sound kind of crazy. Nia must have been worried out of her mind.

"That…looked worse than it really was." Erich spread his arms. "As you can see, I'm fine."

Nia frowned, crossing her arms over her chest. "So this is it? You're leaving?"

Erich picked up his bag. "I'm just moving into Odinshield for a while. Don't worry, I'll still pay the rent here."

Nia rolled her eyes. "It's not about that. I don't need your charity. I can find my own place."

"I know," Erich said. He put his arm around her shoulder and hugged her close. "But I'd like for you to stay here. If anything, just to keep an eye on the place."

When Nia didn't respond, he went on. "Look, this isn't goodbye. I'm just going to work with my brother for a while. I'll only be a couple of miles away and if you ever need anything, just call or come to Odinshield and ask for me."

Nia pulled away and crossed the room as if that small amount of physical distance would make things easier. "I guess there's nothing left to say," she said, her voice cold.

"Listen, this is temporary. I just have to work through some things. That fight set things in motion that I have to deal with."

Nia nodded. "Then you better get to it," she said, glancing pointedly at the door.

Erich didn't move. He couldn't shake the feeling that their

relationship would never be the same. A heavy cloud hung over him like a blanket of dread. He shook his head. He had Sadie. He was back with his Ulfhednar family. Just because he wasn't going to see Nia every day didn't mean the world was going to end.

And yet, the dark feeling remained.

CHAPTER 18

"*W*here's Lover Boy?" Ty asked, putting the SUV in reverse.

"Lover Boy?"

Ty glanced at her. "Yeah. Erich."

Sadie froze. She hadn't realized that Erich's intentions were that obvious. Ty tended to be self-centered. If he knew about their feelings for each other, then everyone else must know, as well. How would Adam react to her dating an employee?

"You okay, doc?"

"Yes, sorry. I hadn't realized that everyone knew about that. We've only eaten dinner together a couple of times."

The color drained from Ty's face. "Oh, yeah. Right. Well... I just asked because..." He cleared his throat. "So where are we going, again?"

Sadie typed the address in the SUV's GPS system. Ty squinted at the map. "Rolenberry Fields. Who lives all the way out there?"

"My foster mother," Sadie said. "I haven't seen her in a

while and…I don't know…I just need to do something normal."

"Fair enough," Ty said as he turned onto the highway. "It must be tough being stuck at Odinshield every day."

Tough was an understatement. While she hadn't had the most exciting life before, she had enjoyed being on her own and getting away from work. She especially missed her biweekly visits to her foster mother. Even after she had aged out of foster care, she had continued to live with Jacki as a roommate until Lauren had become of age. If Jacki hadn't taken her in after she and Lauren had run away, Sadie had no doubt they would have ended up right back with the Children of Light. It's been almost two decades but the memory of her life with the cult still haunted her. At her current age, she would no longer be the Seed of Light. She'd be expected to provide the next generation of alara to be sacrificed to their god. Sadie shuddered.

She perked up as Ty pulled down the long dirt road that led to her foster mother's house. As if by some magical intervention, the surrounding farmland quickly turned into wooded forest and the temperature in the SUV dropped as it drove underneath the trees' shade.

Ty pulled into the empty driveway in front of the small cottage. It sat at the far end of the dirt road and was surrounded by large, looming trees. Sadie had loved to lounge underneath them as a teenager. After living her early years under the watchful eye of the Children of Light, having free, unsupervised time was an anomaly that she had never experienced. She would lean against the trunk and watch the sunlight play along the grass as it broke through the leaves overhead and feel like a feral and wild thing, living free and without a care in the world.

As they approached the house, she inspected the bushes

and flowers that lined the walkway to the front door. Like Wade, her foster mother was from Mti, a land that flourished with massive trees and luscious vegetation. Falling just short of worship, their culture had a close bond with the land, especially trees. It was so close that one could detect the emotional and physical state of someone from Mti by the quality of their garden, and Jacki's garden was healthy and blooming.

Garden inspection complete, Sadie knocked on the door. She turned to Ty.

"My foster mom can be a bit…rambunctious, so don't be alarmed," she said.

Ty smirked. "Thanks for the warning."

As soon as the door opened, Sadie found herself enveloped in a big hug. "Sadie! It's been so long. Where have you been? I haven't seen you in forever."

Sadie giggled and hugged her foster mother. "It's only been a month, Jacki."

Her foster mother pulled away and fixed her with a fierce stare. "That's too long, child," she said, her excitement bringing out her Mti accent. She was dressed in her characteristic house dress, this one a bright orange that clashed beautifully with her deep brown skin. Her dress was cinched at the waist by a leather belt, holding her Mti blade. Unlike Wade, the daggers carried by Mti women tended to be more for show. Jacki's blade had been handed down for three generations. It was secured at her waist in a decorative leather sheath and the handle was inset with emeralds and diamonds that glistened under the sunlight. Despite its beauty, it was still an Mti blade and sharp enough to cut anyone unlucky enough to be at the wrong end of it.

"You haven't called or anything," she scolded. It was then that she noticed Ty standing a few paces behind her.

"Well, who is this?" she drawled. She self-consciously ran

her palm over the short, tight, black curls of her hair, making sure all was in place.

Ty held out his hand. "I'm Tyrell Hannsen, ma'am."

Jacki placed her hand in his like she was a queen expecting him to kiss her ring. "Sadie, you didn't tell me you had a boyfriend. He's handsome," she said, her brown eyes sparkling.

For the first time in her life, Sadie witnessed Tyrell blush. She stifled a laugh. "He's not my boyfriend. He just gave me a ride."

"Well come in, you two. I made a cherry tort last night and it should be chilled by now."

Sadie perked up at the mention of her favorite dessert. She followed Jacki into the cool entrance of her house. It wasn't much, a teacher's salary didn't stretch very far, but it had been enough for Lauren and Sadie. They had shared a bedroom down the short hallway to the right and had stayed up almost every night giggling and telling stories.

Sadie ran her fingers along the small wooden table that had served as their dining table. It was just big enough to fit three chairs, four if you didn't mind bumping knees with your neighbor. Ty made a beeline for the table, plopping his massive body onto the padded seat. Sadie cringed as the chair let out a loud creak, groaning under his weight. Ty didn't seem to notice, his eyes on Jacki as she bustled around the kitchen gathering plates and forks.

She turned from the refrigerator, a large cherry covered pie in her hands.

"I was going to take this to work with me but I'd much rather share it with the two of you. Here, I'll wrap up a piece for you to take back to Lauren." Ty jumped up and rushed to her side, his eyes locked on the pie. She handed him a large slice with a smile.

"Can I have two pieces to take home? I have a friend who

will love it," Sadie said, ignoring the rising heat in her cheeks at the thought of presenting Erich with a slice. Jacki grinned.

"Of course," she said. She put two slices in a plastic container and put on the lid. "Is he your new beau?"

The heat in Sadie's face grew hotter. "Oh. No—"

"Yes," Ty said around a mouthful of pie.

Sadie pressed her hands against her cheeks. While they had met for dinner a couple of times, calling Erich her boyfriend seemed a bit premature. She didn't know what they were and, more importantly, she didn't know how deep her feelings were for him. He was attractive, any woman could see that, and despite his size and, let's just say, proclivity toward aggression, he was sweet and gentle with her. But she had been down that road before. Men tended to flock to her until they found out exactly what they were dealing with. She had the type of baggage that caused them to run in the opposite direction.

"I mean, he's not my boyfriend or anything. He's a friend."

Ty rolled his eyes.

"And when will I meet him?"

"I'll bring him next time I come," Sadie said.

Jacki patted Ty's arm. "Well, I'm glad you came instead. You are such a charming boy." For the second time that day, Ty blushed. Sadie rolled her eyes. Really, it's like the man had never received a complement before.

"Sadie," Jacki said. "Come to the back with me. I want to show you something."

Sadie set her fork down and followed her foster mother. Ty eyed her untouched plate.

"Don't eat my piece," Sadie hissed as Jacki led her into the hallway. Ty took a massive bite and winked at her.

As soon as the door was closed, Jacki wrapped her arms around Sadie in a big hug. "What is going on with you, child?" Releasing her from the hug, she held Sadie at arm's length and looked at her. "You've never bought a friend over before and from looking at him, I can only assume he's someone from the agency you work at. I haven't seen you or Lauren in over a month. What's going on?"

Sadie had never been able to keep anything from her foster mother. Even when she was a teenager, and filled with all of the dramatic and sullen emotions that came along with it, she had always immediately opened up to her. No matter how hard she tried, one look at Jacki's warm eyes had always made Sadie crumble and she would be spilling her heart out over a sweet dessert.

Today was no different. Jacki's eyes widened as Sadie told her about the serial killer who was hunting down alara, how she and Lauren were living in protective custody, the frequent calls from her hometown, and her recent fight with Lauren.

Jacki squeezed Sadie's hands. "You poor thing! What can I do to help? You can stay with my sister," she said, giving her head a sharp nod as if the decision had been made. "This crazy man will never get across the Mti border."

"Thank you so much, Jacki, but I can't take Lauren away from her studies." At Jacki's doubtful look, she rushed on. "The guys at Odinshield know what they're doing. You've seen Ty. They all look like that. No one would dare attack me with them around."

Jacki pursed her lips. "Well, it's reassuring that you're traveling around with a bodyguard, I guess."

"Nothing will happen to me. Don't worry," Sadie said.

Jacki held up a finger and hurried to her dresser.

"I know you are not from Mti, but I want you to have this. It belonged to my cousin. He had no children when he died, so it passed to me." She turned and held up a leather sheath.

Unlike her dagger, the handle was solid black and ridged so that it would fit solidly in her hand. Jacki pulled the handle to reveal a wicked looking blade.

"This is one of his smaller daggers. It's strong but light, so you can wear it under your clothes."

Sadie took the blade and held it reverently. Her vision blurred as she blinked back tears. "Thank you," she whispered. "I know this must be important to you."

Jacki pulled her into a hug.

"I can't help but worry! You're my daughter!"

Sadie almost lost it right then and there. She wished, down to the marrow in her bones, that Jacki had given birth to her instead of her real mother. But since she couldn't change history, having her as a foster mother was the next best thing. Jacki pulled away.

"Come on, girl, let's go back to the kitchen," she said. "That man looks like he could eat me out of house and home."

When they walked into the kitchen, Ty was sitting at the small table, his plate empty.

"Everything alright?" Ty asked. He looked concerned. Sadie mentally kicked herself. She had forgotten that berserkers had enhanced senses. Of course he had heard the entire conversation.

She pasted a smile on her face. "Yeah, everything's great." Ty nodded, his face serious.

Jacki placed the rest of the pie in a circular plastic container and secured the lid. "Here, Tyrell. Why don't you take the rest home for later." Never one to turn down good food, Ty took the container and gave Jacki a hug. She laughed as he lifted her off of her feet with one arm.

"Can you adopt me, too?" he said, setting her down gently.

"Of course," she said with a laugh. "You can come over any time."

After saying her goodbyes, Sadie walked to the SUV with an extra spring to her step. Sometimes feeling the unconditional love of a parent was all you needed to chase the storm clouds away.

CHAPTER 19

*E*rich arrived just as the morning sun was beginning to stream through the conference room windows. Unlike Wade, Adam liked to have his meetings at a reasonable hour, giving Erich the chance to once again take advantage of Odinshield's state-of-the-art gym and fully stocked fridge. He took a gulp of his bottled water as the rest of the guys found seats around the conference room table.

After everything that'd happened since he'd returned, he was beginning to hate this room.

"We've received a missive from Wolveshire," Adam said, holding up a thick piece of card stock, embossed with the Ulfhednar clan seal. For such a rough group of men, the Head Council loved to flaunt their extravagant taste. All of their letters were drafted on the best material and hand delivered via courier. Then again, it's not like they were living a rustic life at Odinshield. Erich took a sip of his imported vitamin water.

Adam looked like he'd rather be doing anything but this. He locked eyes with Erich and, in his typical blunt fashion, said, "The Frelshednar have challenged Erich to a holmgang and the Head Council has approved the challenge."

Erich's jaw dropped. "On what grounds?"

"On the grounds of familicide."

Erich's mouth slammed shut with an audible click. The room was silent as he put two and two together.

"So those fuckers attacked me and then had the nerve to petition the Head Council for a holmgang, as if they are the wronged party?"

Adam nodded. "We have seven days."

"This is bullshit," Erich said. "Those guys tried to kill me. How in the hell can they challenge me? Why would Wolveshire approve it? It's ridiculous."

Adam looked tired as he rubbed his face. "I've been on the phone with them all morning. The Frelshednar deny attacking you. They claim the thugs acted on their own."

"Bullshit," Erich repeated.

Wade cleared his throat. "Even if they didn't attack him on purpose, the fact of the matter is that Erich was attacked and he defended himself. How does that qualify for a grievance?"

"Because one of the victims was a berserker. Even if the guy deserved it, Erich still broke the treaty between our clans," Adam said.

"So let me get this straight," Brandt said, his face tense. "Because of our own fucking treaty, a Frelshednar can start shit with us and if they happen to die when we defend ourselves, their kin can legally challenge us to a fight to the death?"

"So what's the point of this treaty?" Ty said. "The Frelshednar are a bunch of clowns, they obviously can't win against us in a fight. They could start a fight knowing that we can't really pound them into the dirt. Why would Wolveshire create rules that limit us and give them power?"

"Because it's the honorable way to function," Stefen said. He held up his hands in a placating gesture to calm Ty's protests. "Listen, I don't like it either. I'm just telling you what is written in the Ulfhednar doctrine. We are Ulfhednar and we live our lives with honor and discipline."

"Which means we have to put up with this bullshit," Ty muttered.

"Of course, they could have approved the holmgang to get on the Frelshednar's good side," Wade said, his face thoughtful. Everyone stared at him.

"Why, the fuck, would we need to be on their good side?" Ty asked

"Think about it," Wade said. "As two separate clans, we are fractured. Weaker. We would be much stronger if every berserker was on our side instead of fighting against us."

Stefen nodded. "That makes sense," he said, ignoring Ty's derisive snort. "Especially with this new supe. We will be fighting two wars at the same time."

"Well, agreeing to the holmgang isn't going to help," Erich said. "I'm not worried about some Frelshednar schlub. I'll kick his ass and then we can go about our lives." He wasn't boasting, just stating a fact.

Adam looked at the letter. "Unfortunately, it's not going to be that easy," he said. "Because the insult was against the entire clan, they have the right to choose their fighter. They chose Liam Nilsen."

All the air seemed to leave the room. Liam Nilsen wasn't a mindless grunt like the rest of the Frelshednar. Unlike the others, he came from a long history of fighters and had extensive experience in hand to hand combat..

"Shit," Ty breathed, rubbing his hand through his hair. He shot a pitying glance at Erich.

"This changes nothing," Adam said. "The Head Council has approved, so we must answer the call." He pointed at

Erich. "You'll train with Tyrell every day, and Ty, I want a daily report of his progress."

When Erich opened his mouth to protest, Adam held up his hand to silence him. "He's the best fighter out of both clans."

Erich couldn't argue with that. Out of all of them, Wade with his knives was the deadliest, but when it came to hand to hand combat, Tyrell always bested his opponent. He could put a man on his back without breaking a sweat.

Ty smirked. "I'll be happy to teach Erich how to fight."

Erich rolled his eyes.

Adam tossed the letter onto the table and folded his arms to address the room. "The next point of business. We're not any closer to figuring out what type of supernatural is killing alara. I'm sure the doc would appreciate it if we hurry up so that she can go back to her regular life."

At the mention of Sadie, Erich straightened in his chair. All thoughts of his pending fight fled his mind.

"It has to be the bloodborne," Wade said. "One of them must have survived The Great Hunt and has come to Triton City for some reason."

Stefen nodded. "All of the evidence seems to be pointing in that direction."

Adam dropped his gaze, his face thoughtful. He shot a glance to his brother. "Erich, what do you think?"

It took all of Erich's focus to hide his surprise. Before he had decided to live as a civilian, he had been Adam's right hand man. His number one. That had not been the case, since he'd been back. It was understandable, but it still rubbed Erich the wrong way. Having Adam ask for his opinion point blank felt like old times. Erich cleared his throat to hide his emotion.

"Wade's right. Even if this isn't a bloodborne, it's definitely acting like one."

Adam tapped his fingers on the table. "Stefen, continue your research but focus on the bloodborne specifically." Stefen nodded, his eyes already unfocused as he plotted his next steps. Adam turned to Wade.

"See if the coven knows anything," he said. At Wade's nod, he continued, "And talk to your people back home. Maybe they had a run in with the bloodborne back during the Blood War."

Wade froze, staring hard at an invisible speck on the table. Adam cleared his throat.

"Wade?"

Wade startled. "Yeah, I'm on it."

Adam stood and put a hand on Wade's shoulder. "Good man. You know I wouldn't ask this of you if it weren't important."

Erich shot Wade a sympathetic look. While Wade still followed Mti customs, he had been ostracized over a decade ago. Reaching back to them was going to be hard for him.

As everyone filed out of the conference room, Erich immediately headed to the elevators. As usual, his every thought was on his boratai. All of the talk about the blood-borne made him want to see her even more, if anything just to make sure she was alright. He didn't know what he expected to happen to her within the walls of Odinshield but it seemed like he always needed reassurance that she was healthy and in one piece.

The sound of Erich's boots striking the linoleum created a rhythmic beat as he walked down the hall, only pausing as he held his watch against the keypads leading to Odinshield's medical wing. Erich strode into the medical clinic. The room was saturated with Sadie's tantalizing scent of lavender and vanilla. Unsurprisingly, all of the beds were empty. With this issue with the bloodborne, they hadn't been running their usual night runs. The supernatural dregs of society must be enjoying their newfound freedom.

"Doc, you in here?"

Erich felt her approach long before she walked through the door leading from the back offices. As she drew near, all of Erich's stress melted away. He moaned softly as his muscles relaxed and the tangled mess of anger that always simmered just below his skin dissipated. His limbs felt like jelly by the time she entered the room. As usual, she was dressed practically in blue scrubs and white sneakers. Her honey brown hair was pulled back into a loose bun, allowing stray locks to escape and hover around her face. She wasn't wearing her glasses, so he had an unobstructed full view of her deep brown eyes that were framed by long thick lashes. When she caught sight of him, her concerned frown shifted into a smile. Erich's heart leapt in his chest.

"Erich," she said. That's all. Just his name. Erich grinned.

"Hey, doc."

"Is everything alright?"

"It is now," he said. He could feel the goofy grin on his face and forced his features to relax to something resembling a normal adult male.

A small frown formed between Sadie's eyes as she crossed the room. "You sure? You're acting different." She held her hand, palm down, against his chest. Her brown eyes were distant as she used her alara powers to check his body. He was fine, of course. Better than fine actually now that she was near, but he wasn't about to tell her that. He'd do anything to keep her touching him. He almost moaned out loud when she ran her hand through his hair so that she could touch his scalp.

"Well, you seem fine. Your vitals are actually very good for a berserker," she said, taking a step back.

"It's because of you," he said. He immediately regretted it

153

as a look of confusion flitted across her face. Damn. Even his tongue was loosened around her. If he wasn't careful, he'd be blurting out all of Odinshield's classified secrets.

"I mean, because we have the best doc."

Sadie smiled and rolled her eyes. "It's kind of early for dinner and you're not injured. What's going on?"

Erich crossed the room and sat on the examining bed furthest away from her with the hopes that a little distance would clear his head. It didn't work.

"I wanted you to hear this from me first," Erich said.

"Now I'm getting worried," Sadie said. "What is it?"

"You know those guys in the alley? The ones who jumped me?" At Sadie's nod, he continued. "Apparently, one of them was related to a member of the Frelshednar. They've challenged me to a holmgang."

"What's that?"

"It's a fight to the death."

Sadie frowned. "What? Why?"

"It's a way to get compensated for being wronged."

"It's barbaric!" Sadie said.

"Yeah, hello? Have you met us?" Erich immediately regretted his tone when Sadie narrowed her eyes. This was not how he wanted this to go. "Listen, I don't have a choice. If I don't do it, I admit guilt and could be ostracized."

Sadie closed her eyes and shook her head. "Wait, so these guys jumped you and you defended yourself. How were they wronged? If anything, *you* were wronged."

Erich nodded. "That's exactly what I said! But Wolveshire sees things differently."

"Well, you're not going to die. I'll be there to heal you—"

"Absolutely not!" Erich roared. Sadie jumped, her hand instinctively going to her throat. Erich held out his hands. "I'm sorry. I didn't mean to yell."

Sadie fixed him with a piercing glare. "I intend on being there. As the unit's doctor, it's my duty."

"You can't," Erich said. "No outsiders can be in attendance. It's tradition. Besides, I don't want you anywhere near the Frelshednar."

Sadie patted the side of her waist. "I can take care of myself. I have my stun gun."

Erich chuckled. "Doc, that might stop one berserker for a couple of minutes on a good day. The whole Frelshednar pack will be there." When Sadie didn't look convinced, he tried a different tactic.

"Look, apparently, the guy I'm fighting is one of the best. If you're there, I will be distracted. I can't protect you and fight this guy at the same time."

"Is there any way out of this? Maybe you can write the Head Council—"

"If I don't show up, I'll be banished. My own brother will be forbidden to talk to me. As will you because you're affiliated with Odinshield."

Sadie just stared at him, her lower lip trembling. With a soft curse, Erich crossed the room and took her into his arms. She yielded immediately, wrapping her arms around his waist.

"Don't worry. The Frelshednar are a bunch of animals. They lack discipline. I'll win this fight easily and will be back in no time."

"You'd better," she whispered.

It was at that moment, as Erich held his boratai in his arms for the first time, that he realized that she truly was the most important person in his world. He cursed the Frelshednar for putting him in this position. For even giving her the idea that he may be taken from her. Despite the nearness of his boratai, his beast woke up. It hungered for blood and flesh. Erich grinned. Someone was going to pay.

CHAPTER 20

*T*he Seed of Light tucked a stray lock of her dark hair under her white veil. Purity. Covered from head to toe in white linen, she sat on the hard wooden bench, not moving a muscle as she prepared to give her offering to Sabien, Keeper of the Holy Blood. She took a deep breath and released it slowly, allowing her muscles to gently relax. Her hands fell open, palms up, as they rested on her knees. Someone held a small glass in front of her mouth. She tilted her head and allowed the thick liquid to coat her tongue before swallowing. Her body slumped against the wall, her mind developing a delicious fogginess. She thought of Sabien. Her lord. Her protector. Her heart swelled as she thought of the offering she was about to give to him.

"It is time, child." Her father lifted her off of the bench, but she could barely feel his arms under her back and legs. She floated. She was flying. What a gift!

Her father set her down, placing her small right elbow on the arm of the wooden chair. He pulled up the sleeve of her robe. The bruise was almost completely healed. Sabien will be pleased. She noticed that the congregation, who stood together in a dark mass, had grown. Standing shoulder to shoulder, the flickering candle-light creating pretty diamond-like flashes on the plastic buttons of their jumpsuits. More people were coming to the light. Sabien be praised!

The Children of Light stood still, no one daring to move or make a sound. No one daring to displease Sabien.

The contents of the tray rattled as her father gathered the supplies he would need. The noise sounded funny to her ears. Softer than it should be, like the world was wrapped in cotton. The needle glistened as the candlelight flickered against the polished metal. Her father turned her arm so that its white underbelly was exposed and pushed the needle into her skin. It should probably have hurt, but she felt nothing as she watched the red blood flow down the tube and into the white bowl. The Children of Light moaned as the Seed's blood dripped into the bowl. Some cried, bringing their hands to their face to wipe their tears.

The Seed of Light smiled. Her offering will bring great joy to Sabien and plant more Seeds upon this world.

Her father removed the needle from her arm and brought the bowl to the altar. The Children of Light had built the altar centuries ago. The sides were made of polished stone, still light grey after all these years. She assumed the top used to be grey, but years of blood offerings by the Seeds that came before her had stained it with permanent brown streaks.

Her father poured her blood upon the altar, chanting the words that Sabien liked to hear. The congregation answered, their voices loud and rapturous. Her mother approached the altar, her white robe bright against the flickering candlelight. The Vessel of Light. She threw up her hands, wailing the words that Sabien liked to hear. The congregation answered her. Her mother cried, asking Sabien for another blessing. The congregation answered. Her mother implored for a full womb. The congregation answered.

Her mother bent and lapped up the blood that had pooled into *the center of the altar. Red splotches bloomed like flowers on her white robe. She moaned and convulsed on the altar as the blood entered her body. The congregation moaned and rocked back and forth. Some called for Sabien to fill her womb.*

A man, naked but for the gold mask upon his face, approached the altar. He stood behind her mother. He reached down to lift her robe.

The Seed of Light was lifted out of the chair. Her father carried her to the backroom as her mother moaned and shrieked upon the altar. Her father laid her on a soft bed and bandaged her arm. He gave her a sweet drink.

"Sleep child," he said. "Rest so that you may have the strength to bless us with the gift once more."

He kissed her forehead before moving toward the door. The Seed must have made a noise because he looked back and smiled. "All hail the Seed."

Sadie woke with a gasp. It took her a second to recognize her surroundings. Odinshield Protective Agency, posh apartment, fifth floor. She leaned over and turned on her bedside lamp.

She hadn't had that dream in years. Dream? More like a memory. She absentmindedly rubbed her fingers over the small scar on her inner arm. While most people had spent their Sunday's going to church or relaxing, she had been busy having her blood drained and used for rituals. It's amazing that she turned out so well adjusted. More or less.

With a sigh, she sat up and rubbed the sleep out of her eyes. After taking a moment to collect her thoughts, she climbed out of bed and headed into the kitchen to get a bite to eat before going down to the clinic. While being in hiding was an adjustment, her commute was way shorter than it used to be. That's a plus, at least. Munching on her toast, she scrolled through social media posts on her phone. She normally didn't pay much attention to gossip and drama that prevailed on those types of sites, but with her life the way it was at that moment, she welcomed the distraction.

After reading about the overnight antics of the superstar bad boy of the month, she stood to put her dish away. The dinging of her phone caught her attention. She picked it up and froze. Her hand shaking, she read the message again.

My dearest daughter. All hail the Seed. We have had many improvements since you have abandoned us, but we still need the Seed of Light for our family to be complete. Please, daughter. Come back to us. You owe us that much. I would hate for this to escalate further.

How did they find her? Her mind flashed to all of the wrong numbers that she had been getting recently. She normally let them go to voicemail. The only message they would hear would be the generic computerized voice asking them to leave their number. Did she accidentally pick up her phone without realizing it? Her throat felt tight and she swallowed hard. Did they know where she was? Taking deep breaths, she sat back down and held her head in her hands.

There was no doubt about it. She was going to have to go to Adam with this news. Even though she was here due to the monster hunting alaras, he needed to know that the Children of Light had found her. At this moment, she needed the protection of Odinshield from yet another enemy.

Rustling noises in the next room caught her attention. Lauren. What should she tell her sister? Lauren had been just a child when Sadie had taken her away from the cult. She didn't know how much her sister remembered, but Sadie had filled her in on some of the bad things the Children of Light believed in. The blood rituals. The animal sacrifices.

"Wow, you look like you've seen a ghost," her sister said as she padded into the kitchen. Her unicorn slippers perfectly matched her pajamas. Sadie forced a smile onto her face. Lauren could be so innocent sometimes. She hated to kill the mood, but this wasn't something she could hide.

"Actually, I have," she said.

Lauren looked up. "What do you mean?"

Sadie held up her phone. "I just got a text, from my father."

Lauren walked over and took the phone from her. Sadie watched her eyes as they moved back and forth, reading the message. With a deep breath, Lauren handed the phone back.

"Okay, this doesn't mean anything."

Sadie's mouth dropped open. How could Lauren be so calm about this? "What do you mean? The Children know where I am?"

Lauren shook her head. "How do you know? All this proves is that they know your phone number."

Sadie sat back. Her sister was right. Nowhere in the text did her father say he know where she lived. Besides, even if he did, there was no way he'd know she had moved into Odinshield. The text had so unnerved her, that she wasn't thinking clearly. "That's true. But still, this is still freaking me out a little."

Lauren nodded and headed back into the kitchen. "You're not wrong about that. What are we going to do?"

"The first thing we're going to do is tell Adam. He needs to know."

Lauren smiled. "Why don't you just tell Erich. He seems to be your personal body guard now."

Sadie flushed. "He's using his personal time to help me, yes. But he's not my official bodyguard or anything."

"I've seen the way he looks at you. He wants to be your

official something," Lauren said with a laugh. "Boyfriend? Lover?"

Sadie pressed her hands against her warm cheeks. How did this conversation turn to her love life? It was true that Erich seemed to enjoy her company, but he hadn't even kissed her. Goddess knows he'd had the opportunity. Perhaps he was waiting for her to make the first move.

Sadie shook her head and stood up. "Anyway, let's get back to the real problem here. The Children of Light."

"They really scare you, don't they," Lauren said, her voice soft.

Sadie shuddered. There wasn't much on this earth that scared her, but going back to her role as the Seed of Light was the second to the top of the list. Her biggest fear was becoming the Vessel of Light. Her mind flashed to her mother, leaning over the bloody altar as an anonymous man approached. Now that she was an adult, she would be expected to be the vessel that Sabien used to replenish his blood supply. She would be the one expected to give birth to the next Seed.

Her thoughts flashed to her sister. Lauren was nineteen and also the daughter of the Vessel of Light. Although not an alara herself, the gift was in her genes. There was a good chance that she would also be used by the cult to breed more alara.

"Yes, Lauren," Sadie said, her mouth frozen and barely able to form the words. "And if you knew what I know, you'd be scared too."

Sadie hit send and tossed her phone onto the couch cushion and took a sip of her coffee. Decaf this time. The last thing she needed was caffeine streaming through her bloodstream and making her jumpier than she already was. Her parents didn't know where she lived. She should take comfort in that, but there was a small part of her mind that questioned that logic. It's not entirely impossible that they could have seen her leave her apartment with Wade and Ty and followed them to Odinshield. They could be watching the building right now.

She glanced at the window and resisted the urge to go over and snap the curtains shut. She shook her head and took a sip of her coffee. Now she was really being paranoid. If memory served, her parents were not the most tech-savvy people in the world. They definitely weren't the type to be able to conduct surveillance on a company like Odinshield without being detected.

A sudden knock startled her so badly, she spilled coffee all over her hand. Cursing she rushed to the kitchen and rinsed her hand under cold water. The knock sounded again, this time more insistent.

"Sadie, are you there?" Sadie's heart did a little flutter at the sound of Erich's voice. Forgetting her anger, she ran her hand through her hair and hurried out of the kitchen. After a few steps, she forced herself to slow down. Berserkers have excellent hearing and the last thing she wanted was for him to know that she was scurrying to see him.

Oh the games we play.

She opened the door and forced her cheeks to relax into a semi-neutral smile. Erich was leaning against the doorframe and as soon as she opened the door, his eyes flicked to the room behind her as if he was surveying the environment. His hair and shirt were soaked with sweat and his blue eyes sparkled against his flushed skin. It was obvious that he had been working out when she had texted him saying they needed to talk. She hadn't expected him to drop everything and immediately run up there, but a part of her was kind of thrilled at the idea.

"I wasn't expected you so soon. We could have talked later."

Erich smiled down at her. "No biggie. I checked the clinic and you weren't there, so I figured you were still at home."

Sadie flushed and stepped to the side to let him in, trying not to stare at the way his shirt clung to his body. She had sent that text less then five minutes ago, which meant he must have sprinted to the clinic and then sprinted back upstairs.

Erich walked to her kitchen and poured himself a glass of water. "What do you want to talk about?" he asked, leaning against the counter.

Sadie headed into the living room and grabbed her phone. "I got a text message from my parents."

Erich took a drink of water and nodded. "Okay."

Sadie smacked her forehead. "Oh yeah, I forgot you don't know about them."

Setting the drink down, Erich pushed off of the counter and crossed the room. "Let me see the message."

Erich's face grew stormy as he read the message. "I don't like that threat at the end," he said. "We're going to go downstairs and get you an Odinshield phone. They're traceable only to us." Erich read the message again. "What's this "Seed" business?"

"That's…I should probably just tell you all of it," Sadie said with a sigh.

Erich nodded, his eyes serious as he sat on the Great Big Boil. Sadie sat next to him, for once taking comfort in its deep cushions. This was the moment she dreaded. In the past, learning about her history was a sure way to scare a guy off. But she didn't really have a choice. If Erich was going to protect her, he had to know everything.

A small part of her actually wanted him to know it all. She was tired of the secrets. Tired of the shame. At least now, she'd know if he was going to stick around or not.

So she told him everything. How she grew up in a cult that worshipped the blood god, Sabien. How they used her blood for rituals once her alara powers became known. How she used to have a brother who was killed in a ritual because they drained too much. He was silent through it all, his eyes stony and his lips pressed in a straight line.

"So how did you get away?"

Sadie almost cried at the softness of his voice that totally contradicted the angry look on his face. Hope flared in her heart.

"When Lauren was just a toddler, they were already testing her to see if she was an alara," she said. "Just the thought of her little arm being drained…I couldn't take it, so I took her and ran away. We ended up in the foster system and my foster mom took us in."

Erich nodded. "Yeah, Ty told me about her. Good pie."

Sadie smiled. "The best pie. I wish I could see her more often."

"I'll take you over there whenever you want. I'm sorry I missed it the first time."

They were silent, each in their own thoughts until Erich gently took her arm in his hand. He rubbed his thumb over the raised scar on her inner arm.

"They drained your blood," he murmured.

Sadie drew a shuddering breath and tried to ignore the sparks of electricity that his touch was sending all over her body. If he noticed the effect his touch had on her, he didn't say anything.

He suddenly gripped her fingers and pressed a kiss against the back of her hand.

"Go get dressed," he said. "We need to talk to Stefen and get you a new phone."

Swallowing the lump in her throat, Sadie headed toward her bedroom to change. This was a first for her. She had told a guy about her past and he didn't run away. In fact, he was helping her and protecting her. It was a new experience and for the first time in her life, she felt hope.

CHAPTER 21

*L*ife moves in slow motion when you are being choked out. It really gives you time to think. Time to weigh your past decisions and judge all of the actions that brought you up to that moment. And then, right when you are about to blackout, you get a little surge of adrenaline. Your body's last-ditch effort to survive. Then, if you're lucky, you drift off into nothing where all pain and all panic disappear.

Erich was not so lucky.

"You got soft, man!" Ty yelled as he rolled to his feet. Erich laid sprawled on the mat, forcing lungfuls of air into his body. He had been training with Ty for almost a week and always seemed to end up in this position.

"I...just...need to...get back...into it," Erich said.

"You better do it quick," Brandt said from the sidelines. He took a sip from a flask before slipping it into his pocket.

Ty smirked at him. "Are we day drinking now?"

Brandt shot him the finger. "I think we have other things to worry about, like how our golden boy here is about to get his ass kicked by a fucking Frelshednar."

Erich rolled onto his knees and sat back on his heels. "I'm not going to lose," he said. "I may have been gone but I kept in fighting shape."

"You spent the last seven years fighting pansy-ass humans," Ty said. "This guy your fighting? He's spent the last seven years fucking bitches and killing wild animals for sport. Get your fucking head in the game."

"Let's see it again," Brandt said. "And this time, set your feet back when Ty tries to take you down."

The two men squared up across from each other. Erich kept an eye on Ty's waist, ready to respond at the first sign of movement. As soon as Ty shot forward, Erich widened his stance. He dug his feet into the mat as Ty pushed against him. Without warning, Ty shifted his body and wrapped his leg around Erich's. Once again, Erich found himself on his back. Ty straddled him and proceeded to smack each of his cheeks with his open palm.

Like a bitch.

"Stop slapping me!" Erich roared.

"Then get good," Ty retorted, smacking Erich on the forehead. "Stay calm or you're going to lose, every time."

Erich shifted his hips in an attempt to throw Ty off of him. It didn't work. Erich roared in frustration.

"Stay calm and think," Ty said. Erich glanced at Brandt who was watching him with arms folded.

"He can't help you in a holmgang," Ty said. "Think! How do you get out of this?"

Erich took in lungfuls of air, seeking the calm that had retreated deep inside of his mind. Breathing became easier as the panic and rage subsided. In a rush, his mind cleared and his body acted on instinct. He used his foot to trap Ty's leg, and using all of his strength, he pushed down on his opposite foot, effectively forcing Ty off balance. He shoved Ty off of him and rolled to his feet.

"Good!" Brandt yelled.

His praise faded into the air as Ty leapt forward and clipped Erich in the chin. He followed through with a flurry of punches and kicks. Erich brought his hands up and waited, absorbing the hits as best he could. Ty may be the most skilled fighter, but he had a weakness. Endurance. He tended to gas out long before he should.

At the telltale change in his breathing, Erich grinned. Ty waited a fraction of a second too long before throwing his next punch and Erich filled that void with a punch of his own. Ty absorbed it and tried to follow up but Erich had the momentum. He latched onto Ty's shoulder and swept his legs out from under him. Ty went down hard. Erich landed on top of him and, before Ty could recover, swung his arm forward and planted a loud slap on Ty's cheek.

Brandt hooted in laughter. "Yes!"

"Get off me, asshole," Ty said, chuckling.

Feeling victorious, Erich rolled away and on to his feet. "Let's call it a day," he said.

Ty rolled his eyes. "Of course you want to stop when you are winning."

"That's probably a good idea," Brandt said. "The fight is tomorrow and he has to be fresh for it."

At the mention of the fight, Ty sobered. "You got this, man," he said. "Liam's a good fighter, but if you can take me down, you can definitely take him."

"Thanks," Erich said, ignoring the small voice in the back of his head that questioned whether or not he had really taken Ty down. I mean, yeah, he got the best of him a couple of times, but there was no denying that Ty was still the better fighter.

He gave himself a mental shake. He was despairing. Spiraling. He needed to think and clear his mind. Get some perspective. With a quick wave, he headed toward the locker room to shower and change.

Erich pulled his jeep onto the shoulder of the road and turned it off. The silence surrounded him, a heavenly balm for his frazzled nerves. He surveyed the thick woods to his right. Squat Boabo trees, with their characteristic wide trunks, stood amongst the thick foliage of the Mandari and Black Oak trees, crowding out any vegetation that may have sprouted along the forest floor. Only small patches of grass were able to get a foothold amongst the thick roots.

The Red Forest. He had sought refuge here back in the early days of Odinshield. He would wander the woods for hours, listening to the symphony of the wildlife and rustling of the leaves. There was something about the wild strength of nature that soothed him. After a few hours in the Red Forest, even Tyrell's most annoying quips couldn't get to him.

With the holmgang coming up, his strange feelings for Sadie, and his upcoming judgment he was having a hard time controlling his rage. He needed release.

Grabbing his bag, he got out of his SUV and walked into the woods. As he entered the shade of the trees, the temperature dropped by at least ten degrees. There were no trails to guide his steps, not even a game trail. It was as if even the animals knew that this place was meant to be wild and untouched.

Silencing his steps so as not to disturb the animals that lived within the forest, he headed West. He had no specific destination in mind and was just going toward whatever was calling him. The trees crowded around him, forcing him to respect their dominion and go around. Even with his superior strength, when it came to nature, he was as weak as a kitten.

Pausing to take a drink from his water bottle, he looked up at the thick canopy of trees. Boabo trees held all of their leaves at the top, but the other trees didn't, so the forest consisted of random patches of clarity.

Putting his bottle in his bag, he sat and rested his back against a thick Boabo. He took deep breaths, centering himself and seeking the calm peace that he had cultivated during his Ulfhednar training. His limbs grew heavy and his senses expanded, taking in every sound within a half-mile of his position.

He thought he had fallen asleep when he first noticed the orange light off in the distance. He straightened, watching warily as the light bobbed toward him. It moved in a distracted way, bouncing around the trees like it had no sense of direction. As it grew closer, Erich realized that it was more fire than solid light, yet it didn't seem to scorch the trees as it bounced off of them. As it grew nearer, fear rose within him. Not his own. It felt like an external force being pushed upon him. An innocent force. Erich growled, his wolf-like instinct to protect one of his own bubbling out of him. The feeling felt ancient, like the desire of his earliest ancestors were flowing within him. Erich lifted his head and howled his release. A warning to whatever caused the fear that pushed against him.

The fire disappeared. Erich blinked. He didn't move as his senses took in the surrounding sounds of the forest. The fire was gone, but his urge to protect remained. Sadie. He squeezed his eyes shut and moaned as visions of Sadie with her throat slashed flashed in front of his eyes. If he lost this holmgang, who would protect her? As much as he trusted his

Odinshield brothers, they wouldn't be able to protect her like he could. To them, she was just another client and employee.

Adrenaline surged through his veins, making the muscles in his arms and legs twitch with unfocused energy. He would win this fight against the Frelshednar. Losing was not an option.

CHAPTER 22

Sadie flashed Erich a nervous smile as he sat his tray on the table and slid into the booth. His plate was heaped with double portions of Georges' Seafood Surprise. Sadie arched an eyebrow.

"Hungry?"

Erich popped a shrimp into his mouth and wiped his buttery fingers on his napkin. "My fight is tonight," he said, as if that explained why he was gorging himself.

Sadie waited for him to finish. When he continued to shovel food into his mouth, she spoke. "You'd think eating too much would slow you down," she said.

Erich shook his head and grinned at her. "Nothing slows me down, doc."

Sadie picked at her own food. She couldn't understand how he seemed so unaffected by what was coming. A fight to the death. What if he was the one that died?

He obviously hadn't considered that as a possibility. Sadie opened her senses and extended her alara power toward him as best she could with the table sitting between them. His pulse was elevated. He was practically vibrating with positive energy as he shoveled his meal into his mouth. He spoke faster than normal and even his eyes seemed more green than blue. Oh yes, his berserker was probably bursting to come out and only his Ulfhednar training was keeping it contained. While she had witnessed the berserker rage before, it had always been within the context of anger. She had never seen someone in a happy, excitable berserker state. It was downright adorable.

"So what will happen tonight?" Sadie asked. She had hoped to avoid this conversation, but she couldn't help herself. It was easy to ignore the upcoming holmgang when it was days away, but now that the time was near, it had taken over her thoughts.

Erich had eaten the last of his Seafood Surprise and pushed his tray to the side. He eyed her full plate longingly. With a sigh, she pushed it toward him. He gave her a goofy grin.

"Thanks," he said. "Tonight? I fight a Frelshednar."

"I know. I mean, what are your next steps. Are you leaving right after dinner?" Sadie tried, unsuccessfully, to keep the worry out of her voice. If Erich noticed, he didn't say anything.

"We're going to leave here in a couple of hours," he said. "We'll meet up at the edge of the Red Forest just across from Juniper Lane."

He stopped and searched her face. "Don't worry, Sadie. There will be a representative from Wolveshire there to make sure the Frelshednar don't cheat."

"Do you think they will?"

Erich shrugged. "It's hard to say. They don't exactly value following the rules."

"How can you be so calm about this?" Sadie asked, her voice sounding accusatory to her ears. Erich's eyes narrowed. He pushed his plate aside and took her hand.

"Come on," he said. "I want to show you something."

Sadie scooted out of the booth and they walked to the door hand in hand. He held the door open for her. They walked down the long hallway in silence, Sadie taking comfort in the way his hand gripped hers. Although he held her hand gently, she knew that his strength far surpassed any human male. With that strength and his training, he was destined to win in tonight's holmgang.

At least, she hoped so.

They reached the elevator and waited in silence. Once it arrived, Erich pushed the top floor to Adam's penthouse, and used his watch to gain access. Sadie had been to Adam's apartment and office many times. She mentally searched the entire top floor in an attempt to guess what he wanted to show her, but came up empty.

When they reached the top, Erich surprised her by leading her directly to the stairwell instead of Adam's apartment. Once inside, they stopped in front of a metal ladder that led to the roof. She gave him a questioning look.

"We're climbing up that?"

Erich gave her a reassuring smile. "It's worth it," he said. "I used to go up there all the time."

He went up first so that he could push the trap door open. Once on top, he motioned for her to follow. When she reached the top, he took her hand and practically lifted her out of the opening and onto the roof.

Sadie gasped in surprise. Without the surrounding city lights, the night's sky was ink black with only the moon and the twinkling of the stars giving off any light. The stars coated the entire canvas, almost looking like a solid blanket of diamonds. They stood shoulder to shoulder, holding hands and gazing at its beauty.

"Amazing, isn't it?" Erich asked, his thumb stroking the back of her hand. Sadie could only nod.

"To answer your question from earlier, I'm calm because I know that I will have the strength and wisdom of my ancestors to help me. That's the way of the Ulfhednar. A thousand years ago, they figured out the secret to controlling the berserker rage and how to use its power to our benefit."

Sadie squeezed his hand and turned to him. "But like you said, the Frelshednar could cheat. If this isn't a fair fight, how can you know you'll win?"

"I don't. But if I die, it will be an honorable death. I would rather die in battle than because of some accident or illness."

Sadie's breath caught in her throat. As if sensing her pain, he pulled her into a hug. She sighed and melted against him, loving the feeling of his hard body against hers. Sometimes, when she was around him, the world didn't seem like such a scary, cold place.

"Promise you'll come back," she said. Erich chuckled.

"Of course, I'll come back," he said. She pulled away and looked at him.

"Promise me."

He sobered and reached up to cup the side of her face. "I promise," he said.

They stood on the roof top, staring at each other. She couldn't hear anything other than the pounding of her heart. The touch of his hand the only thing that rooted her to reality. His eyes flicked down to her mouth.

"Sadie?" he whispered.

"Yes."

Within a second, he closed the gap between them, taking her mouth in a fierce possessive kiss. All worry fled her mind as he seemed to take over all of her senses. The only thing that existed was the two of them. The feel of his soft lips against hers. The hard planes of his body as he wrapped his arm around her and pulled her against him.

His kiss was bold. Leaving no question as to what he

wanted. His tongue probed the seam of her lips and she parted them to give him access. He didn't hesitate to take what was freely offered and deepened the kiss, gently stroking her tongue with his. His hand snaked around to the back of her head, holding her in place as he explored her mouth. She clung to him, lost in the passion of his kiss.

For the first time, she allowed herself to hope. To believe in the possibility that she could have her own happily ever after. As a berserker, Erich was familiar with unusual things like cults and blood sacrifices. Learning about her past hadn't chased him away. In fact, it seemed to bring them closer.

He pulled away and drew a shuddering breathe as he tucked a stray lock of her hair behind her ear. His expression was torn, as if it was the last thing he wanted to do.

She didn't know why she said it, except that this felt like the perfect time. If he was about to die, no matter how confident he was of the opposite outcome, he should know the truth. He should know that her day began and ended with his face in her mind. He should know that even the thought of his death filled her mind with plots to join him in the afterlife.

"I…" She wet her lips and cleared her throat. "I mean…"

Erich gazed down at her, his brows slightly tilted into a frown. "What is it?"

"I just want to tell you how…what I'm feeling right now but…"

She buried her face in his shirt. Erich chuckled and stroked her hair.

"Whatever it is, it can't be that bad," he said. Sadie took a deep breath, her heart fluttering at the masculine scent of him before pulling back. He smiled down at her, the soft curve of his lips inviting her to more kisses. Sadie cleared her throat and studied the threading on the collar of his shirt.

"I love spending time with you and I want this to never

end. With your fight and everything…I want you to know that you are important to me, and I want us to be together. Like, permanently. You and me…" Sadie whispered, shooting a quick glance at Erich.

His eyes flashed gold and his lips quirked up in a slight smile before he dropped his gaze. With a sigh, he touched his forehead to hers.

"You don't know how long I've been waiting to hear that," he whispered. "But…"

He drew a shuddering breath and took a step away from her. Sadie resisted the urge to fill the silence, instead focusing on calming the pounding beat of her heart. He shook his head, as if trying to forget a bad memory, and looked at her. They stood that way, staring at each other, her brown eyes locked to his gold.

"We should go," he said, leading her to the trap door.

"What?"

He didn't look at her, instead choosing to study the rough rooftop. "I have to meet with the guys soon. Here, I'll help you down."

Just like that. Sadie shivered, whether from the chilly night air, or the sudden feeling of isolation, she didn't know. The lump in her throat made it hard to speak, so she said nothing. She searched his face as he helped her onto the ladder, but he was a blank slate, only focusing on the task at hand. He followed behind her, pulling the door shut above him.

They took the stairs down to the next level and he used his watch to open the door. They walked to her apartment in silence. At her apartment door, she turned to him.

"Please be safe," she said.

"I will," he said, focusing on some point over her shoulder.

With a sigh she held her watch against the keypad. When she opened her door, he turned as if to leave.

"Wait," she said.

He stopped, his back to her. Sadie's heart pounded in her chest. She wanted to go to him. Run her hands along his broad shoulders and force him to look at her. In a perfect world, he would have come back to her with long, confident strides, taken her in his arms and declared his love for her. Instead, he stood in the middle of the hallway, facing away from her, his head down. After a short moment, he seemed to shake himself. He turned to her, his eyes now blue. Sadie straightened eager to hear his next words.

"If you need anything tonight, Stefen will be here." Erich turned and walked away.

CHAPTER 23

ive of the six Ulfhednar of Triton City waited on the edge of the tree line in silence. The Red Forest stood before them, dark and alive as the treetops gently swayed with the wind. The full moon hung bright and heavy, offering its light to anyone dumb enough to be out so late. An unnecessary gift to the men in attendance as being able to see in even the dimmest of light was just one of the many skills bestowed upon them.

"Wade, go check it out," Adam said, his voice soft against the sounds of the forest. Without a word, Wade loped into the tree line and silently disappeared. The warriors waited in silence as he teleported between the trees, the speed of each movement making him invisible to the naked eye. While his father was from the north, his mother was from the southern country of Mti, a country known for its isolationist policies and deadly, knife-wielding fighters. No country dared to attack within Mti's borders due to its heavily forested land-scape and the Mti male's ability to phase between trees. An attacking soldier wouldn't even know an Mti warrior was near until they felt his blade between his ribs.

It wasn't long before Wade returned, appearing suddenly at the edge of the tree line.

"I'll never get used to that," Brandt muttered.

Wade jogged toward the group. "I scouted the site and about one hundred yards around. The Frelshednar are all there and already hyped. No sentries and no one watching their back."

"Typical," Ty snorted.

"And the Black Guard from Wolveshire?" Adam asked.

"Already there with ten soldiers, waiting about twenty feet from the clearing to the East. The Frelshednar don't even know they're there."

"You know what to do," Adam said to the group. "Erich, be prepared. They might try to jump you as soon as they see you."

The men were on high alert as they moved toward the trees. The Red Forest grew uncharacteristically quiet as they silently made their way to the designated area, as if even the animals knew something violent and bloody was about to happen.

Erich took in the surrounding sights and smells, finding calm in the natural strength around him. This wasn't his first fight, but it was his first holmgang. He'd heard about them before, bloody fights that usually ended with someone either dead or seriously maimed.

His entire future depended on what he did this night, but it wasn't just his future that concerned him. How would losing this fight impact Sadie? If he wasn't killed, losing would definitely result in him being banished with no access to any Ulfhednar resources or protection. The Frelshednar could hunt him down and kill him and everyone he loves without suffering any repercussions. Not to mention the enemies he made during his early years at Odinshield.

Dirtbags tended to hate it when he ruined their criminal plans. Go figure.

Sadie's face flashed in his mind. The memory of the hope and joy leaching from her soft brown eyes when she had realized he wasn't going to say he loved her tore at his heart. Erich silently cursed. Kissing her had been a mistake. That one act had taken their relationship to a level his current situation couldn't support.

He did love her, of that he was certain. But holding his tongue had been the right decision. Under these circumstances, it wouldn't have been fair to cross that relationship threshold. Would she still love him if he came out of this disfigured? Would she still love him if he was banished with a bounty on his head?

Connecting her to him before he knew what his future would hold would be a big mistake, especially since he didn't know if the Head Council would allow her to continue working at Odinshield if he lost the fight. They didn't know she was his boratai, and he needed to keep it that way.

It wasn't long before they heard the rabid howls of the Frelshednar. Just before they entered the clearing, Adam held up his fist, signaling for them to stop.

"Stay alert. Brandt, watch our backs."

The brothers nodded. Tyrell stepped in front of Erich and grabbed his shoulder.

"Remember what I told you. Keep your wits about you." Ty smacked Erich's forehead. "If you go nuclear, you...will... lose."

"He's right," Adam said, slapping Erich on the shoulder. The rest of the brothers offered similar words of support. Even Brandt nodded at him with eyes less icy than usual.

Erich took a deep breath and slowly let it out, enjoying the familiar tingle of anticipation he always felt before a fight. He'd been in a lot of fights in his lifetime. They were usually raucous, fun affairs that ended with a couple of bruises or maybe a broken rib or two. But this one was different. This was a fight to the death, or banishment if the Frelshednar member took mercy on him. Judging by the rabid look in their eyes and the way they paced back and forth, beating their chests and growling, mercy was not on the table.

"Ready?" At Erich's nod, Adam turned and took position at the edge of the forest, Wade took up position on his right and Erich and Tyrell on his left. The Ulfhednar clan strode confidently into the clearing.

There will never be a clearer example of the difference between the clans than that moment. The Frelshednar stood in a gaggle, growling and lunging as their enemies drew closer. Some even turning on each other. The true meaning of berserk. Erich smirked as they fought, clawing and punching each other. Good. Let them kill each other. The less of them the better.

In contrast, the Ulfhednar approached as a coordinated group. Years of training giving them the discipline to ignore the raucous taunts of their enemies.

Erich wasn't totally unaffected. The closer he got, the more excited he felt. He shuddered as a cold streak of fire ripped down his spine. His senses intensified as his berserker power engulfed him. The darkness brightened, almost as if the sun was at mid-day and his vision sharpened, allowing him to see the tiniest detail of his enemies. He could not only hear the blades of grass as he crushed them under his boot, but each twig snap as the Frelshednar leapt around. He knew without a doubt that his eyes were gold, but he held fast, calling on his training to keep the beast calm.

Adam stopped a few paces away from the Frelshednar. His men stood a half of a step behind him, forming a solid wall of muscle. Only the golden glow of their eyes gave any indication of the deadly force each man contained with expert self-control.

Bjorn Haralson, the leader of the Frelshednar, stepped forward, raising his hand in an attempt to calm his men. His men ignored him, snarling and lurching at Adam. They stopped short of touching him, however. Erich smirked. Even in their heightened state, they knew that if they initiated contact, all hell would break loose. Under any other circumstance, that would be welcome, but within the rules of a holmgang, it was best to toe the line. The last thing any of the clans needed was to feel the wrath of the elders from Wolveshire.

As if on cue, dark figures melted from the tree line. There were nine of them, all dressed in black. Only the pale color of their skin, or hair in some cases, provided any contrast with their surroundings. The Black Guard.

They were elite soldiers from Wolveshire who served as the elders' personal guard whenever the Head Council left their fortress. Masters of self-control, they could not be provoked. Some wondered if they were even true berserkers. That is, until they saw them in battle. The telltale golden glow of their eyes was the only proof that their superior strength and fighting skills were supernatural.

As they approached, the Frelshednar settled down. Their previous displays of bravado simmering to random growls and mutters. Both clans shifted so that they faced the newcomers.

The Black Guard stopped about five yards away and a solitary member stepped forward. Axel VanHuburt, captain of the Black Guard and direct descendant of the founding father of Wolveshire. He, Adam, and Wade had trained together at Wolveshire. Although Erich didn't know him well, he was aware of Axel's reputation. Axel was well over six feet of solid muscle, and his black hair and blue eyes always made him the center of female attention.

Erich clenched his jaw. Axel may have been respected among the ranks, but his cockiness had always rubbed Erich the wrong way, not to mention the bad blood between Axel and his brother.

Despite their contentious history, Adam stepped forward and gripped Axel's hand in a firm handshake.

"Axel," Adam said. "Welcome to Triton City."

Axel returned the handshake and smirked. "I've heard good things about Odinshield," he said. "Let's hope it stays that way."

Erich stiffened at the subtle insult, but Adam remained unflappable. It took a lot for his brother to show any type of emotion in front of someone outside of his trusted circle. Many have tried, but he always remained calm and if came to blows, he would put a man out of commission with icy efficiency. If he didn't have Odinshield, Erich was sure he'd be a part of the Black Guard or even the Elemental Guard, a post awarded to the most elite Ulfhednar.

He's much more worthy than this asshole.

Axel waited a beat. When he didn't get the reaction he expected, he turned to address the Frelshednar leader.

"Bjorn Haralson," he said. "Is your fighter ready?"

Bjorn stepped forward and crossed his arms over his burly chest. "Aye," he said. "My man is ready to defend his family's honor and avenge the wrongful murder of his dear cousin." He glared at Adam and spat at the ground in front of his feet.

Axel frowned. "Spare me the theatrics. It is my understanding that the cousin was in the process of robbing and assaulting Erich Birkeland." Bjorn's face darkened, but he held his tongue.

"You're lucky the Head Council has approved this holmgang," Axel said. "If it were up to me, I would imprison your entire clan for wasting my time."

The Frelshednar erupted in shouts of outrage. Axel watched them impassively before raising his hand, the universal gesture for "shut the fuck up". That seemed to make it worse as members lunged at him, shouting and cursing at Axel, the Black Guard, and anything else they could think of. Bjorn turned toward his men and shouted for them to calm down, but it was like tossing a glass of water onto a house fire.

As if they received some signal that Erich missed, the Black Guard stepped forward so that they were shoulder to shoulder with Axel. Some hovered their hands over bulging pockets as if resisting the urge to grab a hidden weapon. Erich wasn't the only one to notice. The Frelshednar's impending death seemed to push through the haze of their rage and they settled down, still quietly blustering and muttering to protect their fragile egos.

Axel waited, his eyes fixed on Bjorn in a silent challenge. When the area was totally silent and only the sound of the wind rustling the trees could be heard, he continued.

"As I was saying, I'm not here to hear your sob stories. As the Head Council of Wolveshire's representative, I am here to oversee the challenge between Liam Nilsen of the Frelshednar and Erich Birkeland of the Ulfhednar clan. This fight to the death will result in one winner." Axel paused and glared at each clan. "Under no circumstances will an observer interfere. To do so will result in an automatic loss and banishment of his clan."

Erich's breath hitched in surprise. While he wasn't worried that anyone from Odinshield would interfere, he was surprised at how serious the punishment would be.

Both clan leaders nodded their agreement.

"As you know, with the exception of the Black Guard, no

weapons are allowed, that includes observers," Axel said. With a nod to his men, they split apart and proceeded to pat down those in attendance.

"My men are unarmed," Adam said as Axel patted him down.

"I believe you, but I must verify," Axel said with a smile. He gave a soft whistle to get one of his men's attention. "Hey Cnut, make sure you do a thorough job on the dark one, he likes to hide knives in strange places."

Wade responded with a raised middle finger.

Chuckling, Axel walked over to Bjorn. "I trust you have no objections to being searched."

Bjorn crossed his arms and spat on the ground. "Do what you must. I just want to see that son of a bitch get beat into the ground."

With the search for weapons complete, all in attendance moved aside to form a ring in the middle of the clearing. Holmgangs of the past used to include animal sacrifice and designated battlegrounds marked by stones. Over the centuries, such things were set aside but the main goal remained: fight to the death.

"Fighters, enter the circle," Axel said.

Erich stepped forward and stood toe to toe with his opponent. Liam was an inch shorter than Erich but carried fifty more pounds of muscle. He whipped his head from side to side to crack his neck as his body shuffled with nervous energy. After throwing a few practice punches, he stared back at Erich, his lips folding back into an obscene sneer.

Erich smiled.

Despite his calm demeanor, he wasn't unaffected by the situation. His skin crawled as his body prepared for battle. The rage and bloodlust that always simmered just below the surface pushed against his skin, sharpening his mind. He resisted the urge to lunge forward. He resisted the urge to growl. His hands clenched into fists but he forced himself to remain still and keep his body in the relaxed state he needed to fight with purpose and logic.

Axel raised his arm. "On my mark," he said. Before he could say anything else, Liam lunged forward and swung wildly, his fist connecting with the side of Erich's head.

CHAPTER 24

*S*adie let out a breath as she rubbed her eyes with the palms of her hands. She'd been reading and re-reading the same paragraph for the last few minutes and it was getting to the point where the words were beginning to run into each other. She checked her watch. Erich would be at the Red Forest by now. Did holmgangs start right away, or did the guys hold some sort of ceremony? Was he exchanging blows at that very moment?

Sadie tried to imagine Erich in a fight, but only the gentle, caring man that she loved came to mind. She'd seen a little of his berserker back when he had taken her to Jamison's lab, but that had been more of a protective emotion. He had been a paladin protecting the innocent. She just couldn't picture Erich deep in a berserker rage, not even a controlled one as his Ulfhednar training dictated. She'd only witnessed one berserker in a rage and it had been a savage, frightening sight. Was Erich capable of such violence? She couldn't reconcile that with the gentle man that she knew.

If you need anything tonight, Stefen will be here.

Those had been his last words to her. Right before he was

going to possibly die and right after she had revealed her feelings for him, those were the words he had decided to say. Sadie leaned forward and held her head in her hands. She had been so stupid to tell him how she felt. Is this what people do when they're in love? Make fools of themselves?

And now he was fighting and possibly dying and she wouldn't know about it until the morning. Sadie shook her head. Erich was wrong. It didn't make sense for one of the guys to be put in a life or death situation without their medical support. Maybe that's how they did things in the old country, or whatever, but these were modern times. This was a civilized country and here, people in need had the right to medical care.

Without thinking, she tossed the medical journal aside and jumped to her feet. She stood there, tapping her fingers against the side of her jeans as she considered her next move. Not for the first time, she wished that Lauren was there. This was the exact situation where Lauren's impulsiveness would be just what she wanted to hear.

What would Lauren do?

Sadie smiled. Lauren would have been at the holmgang hours ago. Nothing would have kept her away, yet Sadie hesitated. Always the dutiful one. Always following the rules. And where had that gotten her? At odds with her sister because of the stupid NDA. Locked in this ivory tower, away from Erich who could be drawing his last breath at this very moment.

A picture of Erich flashed through her mind. Erich, on the ground. Bloody. A pulmonary contusion causing respiratory distress. His body straining, fighting against his inevitable death.

"No!" Sadie's voice echoed throughout the empty apartment. Her hands flexed as her alara power flared out of her, seeking to diagnose the mortally wounded version of Erich in her mind. She squeezed her eyes shut in an unsuccessful attempt to block out the bloody mental scene. She took a deep, shuddering breath.

Erich was an elite fighter. He was Ulfhednar. He had been trained since adolescence in the art of using his rage to his advantage. As long as the Frelshednar didn't cheat, he would be victorious.

Sadie's eyes slid to her car keys that were hanging by the door. Having faith in Erich's fighting ability was one thing, but trusting the Frelshednar was another. She didn't know if she had the strength to do either.

CHAPTER 25

The Frelshednar thug followed his punch with a right hook, but Erich was ready for it. He held up his arm to block it and shot out a jab. Liam's head snapped back as Erich's fist connected with his nose. Instead of subduing him, this only served to enrage him and he lunged at Erich with a roar, catching him around the waist. Erich widened his stance to keep himself from being taken down while snaking his arm underneath Liam's head. He brought his arm around to the front of his body, forcing Liam's head to turn. With a curse, Liam released Erich's waist and spun out of his grip. Erich followed with a flurry of punches.

The Ulfhednar side of the circle went wild as Erich drove the Frelshednar back and off-balance. Liam absorbed most of the punches with his forearms as he covered his face. Without warning, he lashed out, his fist connecting with Erich's chin in a brutal uppercut. Erich stumbled back, slightly dazed. Liam took advantage and knocked him to the ground with the full force of his body.

Liam straddled him, locking his arms as he wrapped his hands around Erich's neck. Erich bucked against him, trying to break free, but the weight of his opponent restricted his movement. The Frelshednar's strong grip cut off Erich's air. His sight dimmed as he clawed at Liam's arm. The shouts of the crowd faded to a low muffle as his ears filled with the sound of the blood rushing through his veins. Erich flicked his eyes to the right and locked eyes with his brother. Adam stood with his arms crossed, only the bright golden glow of his eyes revealing any hint of emotion. Erich focused on the golden circles, drawing on his brother's strength as his sight dimmed along the edges of his vision.

Erich jerked as his brother's face was replaced by Ty's furious glare. Ty had jumped in front of Adam and was screaming something. Erich couldn't hear him, his ears only registering the pounding of his heart, but he could read his lips. Ty was screaming the three words that were seared into his brain from a week of brutal training: Stay calm, asshole!

Gritting his teeth, Erich grasped Liam's wrist and elbow and hooked his leg around Liam's ankle, locking him in place. With the last resolve that he had, he bucked his hips, knocking Liam off balance. Erich rolled with him until he was on top and landed a couple of solid punches before Liam kicked him off.

Barely taking any time to gulp in air, Erich got to his feet and landed an open-handed slap on Liam's face.

Bitch slap.

The Frelshednar paused as if he couldn't believe what had just happened before roaring in anger. He rushed at Erich, his armed cocked back, telegraphing his next move. Erich dodged as Liam flailed his arms. With each opening, Erich whipped his arm in and smacked the Frelshednar on the cheek before stepping back. Liam bellowed, the veins on his neck pushing against his skin.

With a guttural yell, he charged blindly at him. Erich landed a kick to Liam's exposed stomach. As Liam doubled over, Erich jumped on his back and wrapped his arm around his neck until the inner bend of his elbow pressed against Liam's windpipe. Liam instinctively reached for Erich's arm, but Erich quickly tightened the chokehold and snaked his other hand behind Liam's head, not only cutting off his air supply but also applying pressure to the arteries in his neck to cut off blood flow to the brain.

Liam clawed wildly at Erich's arm. Erich grinned as he increased the pressure. The smell of the Frelshednar's fear smelled like heaven. Liam jerked his body from side to side, trying to dislodge Erich's arm enough to take a breath. Erich moved with him, smiling as the man's movements became softer, enjoying the feeling of his life force draining out of him. It was heady, like he had just downed a whole bottle of the most potent Sardovian liquor.

A soft gasp. The scent of lavender and vanilla.

Erich's head snapped up. Ignoring the struggling man beneath him, he scanned the tree line, his elevated senses giving him the ability to see the smallest detail in stark relief. She was here. His woman. He saw her peeking out from behind a tree. Her face pale. Her dark eyes wide in fear. Her small hand covering her mouth. A large masculine hand grabbed her arm and pulled her behind the tree.

Erich roared.

Within seconds, Erich tossed the Frelshednar aside and was on his feet and sprinting toward the tree.

Ignoring his brothers' celebratory slaps, Erich ran to the tree line. Brandt had his arm around Sadie's shoulders, holding her in place as he whispered furiously at her. Sadie looked frightened. Without thinking, Erich pushed Brandt in his chest, knocking him a few yards back. Sadie gave a startled cry. Brandt landed deftly on his feet but didn't approach. He held up his hands in a placating gesture. "I was just keeping her out of sight," he said. Erich ignored him and turned to his woman.

"What the fuck are you doing here?" he asked.

Sadie didn't answer, instead she held her hands over his abdomen as if to determine the extent of his wounds.

He pushed her hand away. "Don't," he said, grabbing her arm. "Come on, we're getting out of here."

The raised voices from the Frelshednar silenced any protest she might have made. As Erich pulled her toward the tree line, he glanced over his shoulder. Adam was in the center of the opening, speaking tensely with Bjorn. The Frelshednar leader made little effort in calming his men as they leaped about and snarled at the Ulfhednar and the Black Guard.

As they ran deeper into the forest, Wade appeared at their side. Sadie yelped in surprise. Erich pulled her behind him, his fists up and snarling, but relaxed when he saw Odin-shield's number two.

"I got her, Wade, get back and watch Adam's back."

Wade flipped a throwing knife that had somehow escape their weapons inspection. Erich didn't want to think about where he might have been hiding that thing. "No can do, my friend. I'm here on Adam's orders. I need to make sure Sadie gets out of here in one piece."

Erich turned to Wade, his eyes flashing gold. "Sadie is under my protection," he snarled.

Wade nodded. "I get it, man. Let me rephrase. I'm here to watch YOUR back so that you can get her out of here in one piece."

Erich couldn't argue with that logic. His first priority was getting Sadie to safety and standing around talking was only putting her in more danger. They resumed their fast pace through the trees. When they reached the tree-line, Erich pulled Sadie to the passenger side of Wade's truck. While crossing over to the other side he looked at Wade. Without missing a beat, Wade tossed him his keys.

Sadie was quiet as he pulled onto the highway, which was probably for the best. Remnants of his berserker rage still flowed through his veins, making his skin feel hot and tight. He felt frazzled, like the slightest thing would set him off and with Sadie so close, he knew that violence was not going to be his reaction. He shot a glance over to the passenger side. She sat primly, her hands neatly folded in her lap, just inches away from the tantalizing V of her thighs.

Erich's breath grew ragged and he fought every instinct to pull the truck over and fuck her right on the side of the street. He took a deep breath.

"I'm going to drop you off at Odinshield. Where the fuck was Stefen? He should have been watching you. You are to go in and not leave," he said, his voice sounding strained. He grimaced, hoping she wouldn't notice. They rode the rest of the way in silence with Erich trying to think of anything but Sadie and her luscious thighs. He pulled Wade's truck to a stop in front of the back entrance of the building. They sat in silence listening to the soft patter of the rain hitting the window of the truck. Sadie was the first to speak.

"Did you win?"

"Yeah," Erich said. He risked a glance over to her and instantly regretted it. She was staring at him with large warm eyes. Her lips were wet, like she had just licked them. He looked away.

"Is...is the other guy dead?" Sadie asked, her voice sounding small.

Erich sighed and scrubbed his face with his hand. "No. A couple of more seconds, maybe, but he was still moving when I let him go."

"So, that's good right?"

"Maybe. I have a Thing with the Black Guard tomorrow, so I'll know for sure then."

"A Thing?"

"It's like an official meeting with Wolveshire. That's when they'll tell me the judgment of the Holmgang and... other things."

She didn't say anything, letting the silence hang between them.

"Are you hurt?" she asked. She reached over and placed her hand on his abdomen. It took all of his self-control to not react to her touch.

"You tell me," he said. She shot him a shy smile.

"Nothing permanent," she said. She began to pull her hand away but Erich caught it. She glanced at him, a soft hitch in her breathing. That one sound, just short of a gasp almost drew Erich over the edge. He reluctantly released her hand.

"You should go," he said, his voice coming out rougher than he'd like.

Sadie hesitated, her hand on the door handle. "Do...do you want to come in?"

"I don't need healing, Sadie. I'll be fine."

Sadie wet her lips, Erich was momentarily distracted by the small pink tongue. She shyly glanced away. "I'm not talking about an exam."

Silence hung between them. "Sadie, you don't know what you're asking," Erich said

"Yes, I do."

Erich squeezed his eyes shut. "I don't know how much you know about us, but in the state that I'm in, I need to fight or fuck." Erich looked at her. "And if I go in that building with you, we are definitely not fighting."

Sadie smiled and stepped out of the truck. "I know," she said. She closed the door and walked toward the building.

CHAPTER 26

$\mathcal{T}$he short walk to the Odinshield building was the longest she had ever taken. She listened intently for any sound indicating that Erich was following her. Instead, she could only hear the soft patter of rain falling on the pavement and leaves of the nearby trees.

Sadie held her watch next to Odinshield's all-weather keypad and waited for the sound of the locking mechanism to release. As soon as she stepped into the building, she felt his presence behind her.

With a sigh of relief, she turned around, but before she could say anything, Erich had captured her lips with his in a deep kiss. He walked her backward until her back was against the wall. She melted against him, loving how the hard strength of his body pushed against hers; loving the feel of his hands as they explored her body.

Sadie ran her fingers through his hair, slightly damp from the rain, and gasped as his hand cupped her breast, his thumb stroking her nipple. Her legs felt shaky as lustful heat erupted within her core.

"Erich…"

He broke away with a groan and planted hot kisses along her neck. She shivered as each kiss sent little spikes of electricity down her spine.

Her mind flashed to the first time he had taken her in his arms. It seemed so long ago. Even then, she knew that in his arms was where she was supposed to be, and what was coming was their destiny.

But the hallway was not the right place for what she had in mind. Reaching between them, she pushed against his chest. He moved back immediately, his breath ragged and his blue eyes searching hers. He leaned forward and placed a hand on the wall behind her.

"What's wrong?" He traced the curve of her cheek with his finger. "You don't want to?"

Sadie reached up and cupped his face. "No… I mean yes, I want to."

He pulled back, his eyes tightening in confusion. Heart pounding, she took his hand and led him down the hall. She normally wasn't this forward when it came to sex, instead preferring for her partner to take the lead. But he could have died tonight. If she couldn't have his heart, she would have to be content with whatever he was willing to give. And the heated look in his eyes told her exactly what he wanted to do to her.

As soon as they entered Erich's room, she was back in his arms. They both fumbled around, trying to touch every inch of each other's bodies and take off their clothes at the same time. With what sounded like a mix between a growl and a groan, Erich lifted her off of her feet, her legs naturally wrapping around his waist. He held her like she weighed nothing, taking a moment to explore her mouth with his tongue. The head of his cock pressed against her, hot and hard. She rotated her hips, loving the feel of it gently dipping into her folds. Erich chuckled and slapped her ass.

"Not yet, doc," he said as he gave her cheek a squeeze.

He carried her the few steps to his bed and laid her down gently, like she was made of delicate glass, and covered her with his body. Sadie felt lightheaded as his warmth and scent surrounded her. He smelled like clean air and trees and wild things. She opened her mouth to his probing tongue, returning his kiss with equal passion. With a guttural moan, he dipped his head and explored her body, planting hot fiery kisses along her breasts and down her stomach. Sadie arched her back, moaning as the heat of his breath sent tingles throughout her body.

He latched on to her sex, his tongue moving in lazy circles before flicking across her clitoris. Sadie let out a soft cry as his tongue repeatedly flicked across the delicate nub. He chuckled as Sadie clamped her knees together, locking him in place. She writhed against him, her hips moving in uncoordinated circles until he grabbed them, holding her still so that he could commit his erotic torture uninterrupted. The strength of his grip and the tortuous speed of his tongue was too much. Her legs trembled as hot fire erupted from her core. She gripped the sheets and cried out as the magic of Erich's tongue brought her to release.

Erich kissed his way back up her body, stopping to give extra attention to her breast. She trembled against him as his mouth coaxed orgasmic aftershocks from her sensitive body.

With a shuddering breath, he pulled back, his gaze raking the length of her before looking at her. With his disheveled hair and flushed skin, he looked wild and raw. His bright eyes were green again as he searched her face; questioning. Sadie reached up and ran her hand through his hair. She could feel the heat of his cock pressing against her, seeking entrance. She circled her hips, rubbing against his sensitive skin. His breath caught as his eyes closed in a long blink.

"Sadie…" he whispered.

"Yes."

Erich's eyes flared gold, telling Sadie there was no going back. He captured her mouth in a hot, possessive kiss before slowing pushing into her. Her body was still humming from before and each thrust of his hips pulled a moan of pleasure from deep within her until she was clinging to him, her voice sounding raw and foreign to her own ears.

With a growl, he hooked his arm under her knee and pulled her leg up so that it rested on his shoulder. They both moaned at the sensations from the new angle as he furiously worked his hips against hers. It was too much. Sadie shuddered and trembled beneath him as her body exploded into a toe curling orgasm. Erich pressed his lips to her neck, growling incomprehensible words as his body shivered from his own release.

He held her tightly as they both came down. Keeping most of his weight on his arms, he pressed small kisses along her neck and shoulder. Sadie sighed as she lazily ran her fingers along the muscles of his back. The weight of him was comforting. Like he was a living shield between herself and the rest of the crazy world.

But it was all an illusion.

She had stood on the roof of this building and shared her true feelings, only for him to shut her down. No, this security that she felt was only temporary. Like always, it would be her against all of the crazy things this world would throw at her.

Erich rolled off of her, distracting her from her thoughts. With a sigh, he tucked her into his side. The silence hung between them, comfortable and cozy. Sadie's eyes began to droop as Erich stroked her back with his fingertips.

"We should talk about what was said… before," Erich said.

Sadie kept her eyes down, focusing on the purpling bruise on Erich's side. She suddenly felt cold. The last thing she wanted to do was rehash... before. The time where she had foolishly expressed her true feelings for him, only for him to walk away.

He gently touched under her chin with his finger and forced her to raise her head. She reluctantly lifted her gaze as Erich brushed back a lock of hair that had fallen into her face, the touch gentle and reverent. He settled his hand gently on the swell of her bare shoulder, holding her in place as if he were afraid she would run away. Somehow the bruises on his face made his blue eyes appear bright and electric. Even after the pain of his rejection, he still took her breath away.

"Did you hear me?" he asked, his voice soft.

Erich's gaze dropped to her mouth as she nervously wet her lips. "It's okay," she said. "I shouldn't have said anything. It was unprofessional, and I was just... worried."

Erich made a point of glancing at their entwined bodies before looking back at her. "I think we've gone beyond worrying about professionalism," he said.

Sadie giggled. "Good point."

Erich ran his fingers along her exposed hip, his touch gentle. "So you don't want to be with me?"

Sadie hesitated. "Erich..." The silence hung between them. With the way he was looking at her, his eyes soft and gentle, she was tempted to answer honestly. But the memory of that chilly time on the roof stopped her.

She tried to roll away, but his grip tightened on her hip, stopping her. She pushed against it until Erich reluctantly let her go. She felt his eyes on her as she stood and gathered her clothes that were strewn around the room. Erich followed, pulling out a pair of athletic shorts from a duffel bag on the chair by the bed. She dressed quickly, her fingers suddenly turning to fat sausages as she tried to button her blouse.

Avoiding his gaze, she crossed the room and stopped in front of his small bookcase, looking at the multicolored paperbacks but not really seeing anything.

She felt the heat radiating off of his body and spun around. He had somehow managed to cross the room without making a sound. She yelped in surprise.

"How do you do that?"

He reached out and touched her arm, his hand lingering as if he needed some sort of physical connection.

"Sadie…" His voice was soft. Her name rolling off of his tongue like the prayer of a starving man. He swallowed hard, the muscles in his neck working. Sadie straightened her shoulders. There was one thing she wasn't, and that was a coward. She loved him and she wasn't ashamed of it, even if he didn't love her back.

"Yes, Erich. I do," she said. She held up her hands to stop him from talking. "And you don't have to say anything. In fact, I shouldn't have—"

Sadie gasped as Erich wrapped his arms around her and pressed his lips against hers. She stiffened before melting against him. As he deepened the kiss, she snaked her arms up and wrapped them around his neck. He pulled back and gazed down at her.

"Sadie Carmichael, I've loved you since the first time I set eyes on you," he whispered. Sadie gave a shuddering sigh as her heart did flip flops in her chest.

"Really?"

"Yes," he said. "As soon as I walked through that door, I knew."

He spoke as if such a thing was possible. Insta-love only happened in movies and romance novels. There was no way he had loved her from day one, but she appreciated his attempt at diffusing the situation.

"So you're saying that it was love at first sight?" She chuckled. Her smile faded when she noticed his serious face. "Erich? It was a joke."

Erich pulled away and walked over to his discarded shirt. "There's something I need to tell you."

Sadie's stomach clinched. Here it was, the other shoe that was about to drop. Whenever she found happiness or contentment, something always seemed to come up to ruin it.

"What is it?" she asked, her voice sounding high pitched and thin to her ears. Erich seemed to notice it too because he hurried back to her and took her hand.

"It's nothing bad," he said. "It's just… something about me that you should know." He guided her back to the bed and motioned for her to sit down. With a sigh, he sat next to her, looking straight ahead as if avoiding her gaze.

"What is it?" she asked. "Just tell me."

Erich let out a deep breath. "Do you remember how I acted when we first met?"

Sadie nodded. How could she forget? One second she was greeting her boss and the next, his brother was pressing his strong body against hers. It was one of her favorite memories of him.

"I need to explain why I did that," Erich said. When he didn't continue, she nudged him.

"It's obviously because you were attracted to me," she said.

Erich nodded. "I was… I mean… I am. It's more than that, though. I didn't know it at the time, but you are my boratai."

Sadie frowned. "Boratai. I've never heard of it. What is it?"

"You're my soul mate. My once in a lifetime match.

There's something in my berserker genes that has recognized you as my one true partner. It's like I'm bonded to you and I have no control over it."

"So you don't necessarily love me. You're just attached to me through this boratai bond?"

Erich jumped up and turned to her. "No, Sadie. This is so much more than love. I can't explain it. But the world is a calmer, more peaceful place when I'm near you. You quiet my rage and for the first time in my life, I can feel something other than bloodlust and desperation."

Sadie nodded. "So I make you feel peaceful," she said. The world was a chaotic place for everyone, but that level of chaos was amplified for berserkers. For a berserker to find peace was a big deal. Her heart swelled at the thought of being the one to bring that peace to such a powerful man.

All hail the Seed.

Sadie straightened as the familiar phrase echoed in her ears. Erich pulled back, his eyes searching her face. "What's wrong?"

Sadie drew a shuddering breath. "I make you peaceful," she said. "But not me. Just my presence. My body."

"It's not your body," Erich said, his features pulling into a frown. "It's you. All of you."

He said other things, but his voice came out low and muffled. All she could think about was being consumed. Her body being used for the benefit of others. Of being strapped to a chair. Needles being pushed into the white underbelly of her arm. Her blood, red and thick, flowing into a bowl.

Cool hands touched her cheeks. When had she become so flushed? Erich's worried blue eyes filled her vision.

"Sadie? Are you with me, baby?"

Sadie closed her eyes in a long blink before focusing on Erich's face. "Yes," she said, taking a deep breath. She pushed his hands away and stood. "I'm fine. I just have to think about this."

Erich was by her side in an instant. "I don't know what just happened, but being my boratai isn't a bad thing. I'm not using you for your body."

Sadie touched his arm. "I know. This just brought up something from my past and I don't know how to process it."

As if he couldn't help himself, Erich took her into his arms. As the warmth of his body surrounded her, she immediately relaxed into him. "What was it? Your family? The Children of Light?"

Sadie blinked back tears as she allowed herself to be held and comforted. She'd never felt that way before. It was as if being in Erich's arms could take away all of her problems. The big scary world didn't exist as long as she had her berserker holding her.

But life didn't work that way. Not for her, at least. She was Erich's boratai, just like she was the Children of Light's Seed. They needed her for the betterment of their own lives. Once again, she was a tool to be wielded when her loved ones needed her and then locked away until they had a use for her.

She pulled away and gave Erich a shaky smile. "I should probably go," she said.

"You sure? I don't want to leave things like this."

"No, it's fine. I just have to wrap my mind around this," Sadie said, making a twirling motion around her temple with her fingers.

Erich hesitated a beat before nodding. His face grim. "Okay. I know I sprung this on you pretty quickly. We can talk some more after the Thing."

Sadie smiled, her cheeks feeling warm and shaky. They walked to the door in silence, the warm lust and closeness from earlier now replaced by uncertainty. On a deeper level,

Sadie wished that she didn't feel the way she was feeling. Without her past, she would have probably been flattered to be Erich's boratai. But once again, the Children of Light had ruined her life. Because of them, she couldn't trust. Because of them, she couldn't give of herself fully and without hesitation. Because of them, she could never have the love she so desperately wanted.

CHAPTER 27

*E*rich ended the call without leaving a message on Sadie's voicemail. He took a second to compose himself before turning and walking into the conference room. The rest of Odinshield was just wrapping up from their pre-brief and guys were standing and milling about.

"You ready to go?" Adam slapped Erich on the shoulder.

Erich nodded. "Yeah, I just needed to finish something real quick."

Adam gave Erich a serious look that he probably thought was reassuring. "Don't worry. Axel and I go way back. I know how the guy thinks."

Erich shrugged and moved to the side as Wade joined the conversation. "I'm not worried. I beat that Frelshednar's ass fair and square."

"But you left before it was called," Wade said. "Is that going to be an issue?"

Adam sighed. "I don't know. In the past, a death was required for victory, but the last holmgang was over a hundred years ago. These are different times."

"True," Wade said.

"Hey, you two head out, I'll meet you at the car," Adam said. Without waiting for a response, he headed across the room toward Stefen.

"Let's go," Wade said as he slipped a knife into one of the hidden pockets of his vest. Erich grabbed his arm.

"Hey, I want to apologize for last night," Erich said, lowering his voice. Wade watched him, his brown eyes wide in confusion.

"Apologize for what? You represented Odinshield well. I mean, it got a little hairy there in the end but you turned it around," Wade said. Erich gave his friend a small smile. Despite Wade's size and deadly accuracy with a blade, he rarely took offense and never held a grudge. It made Erich wonder how Wade's berserker gene was awakened in the first place.

"After the fight, when I was taking Sadie out of there. I was a dick to you," Erich said. "I shouldn't have done that."

Wade nodded. "Don't worry about it. You were still high from the fight and you're protective of your girl. I get it."

They headed to the parking lot and got into their vehicles. While any official visit from Wolveshire would normally have occurred in Odinshield Headquarters, the nature of this Thing warranted it being on neutral ground.

Erich and Adam drove to the meeting location in silence, a normal occurrence for the brothers. Adam was never one for small talk. Erich had learned a long time ago that and any attempt at conversation would only be met with one or two-word responses.

When they reached the edge of the Red Forest, they met up with the others at the tree line.

"Wade," Adam said. Once again, Wade jogged to the nearest tree, placed his hand on the bark and disappeared. While they waited, Adam turned to the group.

"If this doesn't go our way, you know the plan," he said.

Every member of Odinshield nodded. Erich struggled to keep his face impassive. There was a real possibility that this could end in a bloodbath, yet his brothers stood by his side. He expected such loyalty from Adam or Wade, but for Ty or the new guys to have his back was surprising. This was true brotherhood.

Wade returned and gave them a thumbs up. "Axel and eight of the Black Guard are in the clearing. One is hiding in the trees as a lookout."

The walk back to the battleground was a lot more cheerful in the middle of the day. Unlike the previous night, the animals of the forest were out and about, making noise as they darted around. A soft breeze rustled the leaves about them and danced along Erich's skin. He tried to relax and enjoy being in nature, but his upcoming judgment weighed on his mind.

The Black Guard were waiting for them. Any sign of the fight the night before was long gone and the area looked welcoming and bright. A good omen. Axel stood in the center of the clearing, his black tactical clothing from the previous night replaced by loose-fitting jeans and a black t-shirt. Adam greeted Axel with a handshake.

Axel turned to Erich. "I see you've recovered from last night."

Erich just nodded. A Thing was an official meeting. As much as he wanted to skip the pleasantries and get to the point, it was best to leave the speaking to his chieftain. Fortunately, Adam didn't waste time.

"What is Wolveshire's verdict of the holmgang?"

Axel looked at the Odinshield berserkers, his gaze seeming to take in every detail and casting judgment. His eyes stopped on Stefen. "Stefen Askelson. I see they finally let you out of your gilded prison."

Stefen remained silent, only giving Axel a small nod.

"Axel," Adam said, his voice holding a note of warning.

Axel crossed his arms, his face grim. "I discussed the fight with the Head Council. The fact that Erich left the match before a determination was made did not sit well with them. He lacked discipline and it reeked of cowardice."

Erich's stomach dropped. At the time, his mind was set on getting Sadie as far from the Frelshednar as he could. He hadn't considered the possibility of his actions appearing cowardly in front of the Black Guard.

"Discipline?" Adam asked. "What about the Frelshednar? We all saw him throw that sucker punch before the match was started."

Axel sneered. "He's a Frelshednar. What do you expect? We are Ulfhednar. Discipline is expected at all times, and Erich showed a distinct lack it. He acted in a manner unworthy of the Ulfhednar."

"So what is the verdict?"

Axel stared at Erich, a small smirk on his face. He was enjoying this. Erich clenched his fists, wanting nothing more than to smash them into his teeth.

"I couldn't help but notice your reaction to the woman at the holmgang. With the recent discussion about berserkers and boratai, I can't help but wonder if that was the woman in question," Axel said. Erich crossed his arms.

"What business is it of yours," Erich said, breaking protocol by speaking. "You're here to deliver the Head Council's judgment, what is it?"

Axel frowned. "I think you misunderstand," he said. "Yes, the Head Council has come to a judgment, but that is contingent upon my own observation of your behavior and self-control. If I don't feel you are fit to represent the Ulfhednar, then you will spend the next few years up at Wolveshire undergoing rehabilitation."

Erich showed no emotion, only the bulging muscle from

his clenched jaw giving any indication of what he was feeling. Axel smirked. Wade stepped between them.

"I think we all understand why you are here, Axel. Let's just get to the judgment, okay?"

Axel shrugged. "Fine, but keep in mind that the final decision rests with me. The head council has given me the authority to override their judgment. I was a witness to Erich's embarrassing display of cowardice. He left the field of battle to chase after a woman. All I hear at Wolveshire is that Odinshield is the cream of the crop. The vanguard organization that all other chapters seek to emulate. Yet, one of their founding members chose a woman over his honor."

Erich ground his molars together to keep himself from cursing the cocky bastard out. He took a calming breath as Axel glanced at him. This was a test, of course. It was an evaluation of his self-control. Unfortunately, he was pretty close to failing.

"The fight was over and Erich had clearly won," Adam said. "The rules of holmgang require a death. Would you rather he had killed the guy and reignited the war between the clans?"

Axel grinned, his answer obvious to all present. Without a word, he turned to stand amongst the Black Guard, as if he would need their protection. Erich's stomach dropped. That could only mean one thing. Rehabilitation. He glanced at his brothers. Six against ten. Not good odds.

"Wolveshire's initial assessment is that Erich Birkeland defeated Liam Nilson in a fight for honor. The spirit of the holmgang has been met and Erich's honor is restored."

Erich let out a breath that he didn't know he had been holding. He could sense the relief from the men around him. It wasn't until he noticed that Adam was still watching Axel, his shoulders tense, that he remembered that there was more to come.

Adam crossed his arms. "And what is your assessment?"

Axel smirked. "You're right to be concerned." He turned to Erich, holding him in place with his fierce gaze.

"My assessment is that Erich Birkeland brought shame upon the Ulfhednar last night. That fight should have ended within the first minute, yet he allowed himself to be brought down and almost choked out. Not only that, his reaction to his boratai revealed a potential weakness to our enemies."

"They may be our enemies, but they are also berserkers. They could potentially have boratai, too," Adam said.

"Do you really think those animals would take the time to figure that out?" Axel asked, his features twisted in a snarl. "They'd just claim the bitch and go on with their useless lives." He turned back to Erich. "But to leave a fight, a holmgang, to chase after a woman..." Axel shook his head. "The Frelshednar are stupid, but Bjorn is not. He knows something is up. I suggest you keep a close eye on your woman, Erich. She could easily become a pawn in the war between the two clans."

Erich almost laughed at the irony. If it were to come between the bloodborne or the Frelshednar, the Frelshednar were the least of his worries.

"Still," Axel said. "If what is currently known of the boratai bond is true, to remove Erich from Odinshield and send him to Wolveshire for rehabilitation would also deprive you of your doctor. With this bullshit that's going on with the bloodborne, you can't afford to lose a fighter, let alone your medical support."

Erich kept his face blank, but his mind was rolling. Would Sadie go to Wolveshire with him? He didn't think he'd be able to function without her, but she obviously didn't feel the same type of bond as he did. She could decide to move halfway around the world if she wanted to. Erich's gut clenched at the thought. Her strange behavior last night and the fact she wasn't answering his calls didn't bode well. Could she be packing up and leaving at this very moment?

Erich took a deep breath to calm his racing thoughts. It didn't work.

"Due to the current situation with the bloodborne, I will not deprive Odinshield of necessary elements. I concur with Wolveshire's judgment." Axel stared at Erich. "But know this, Erich Birkeland. Wolveshire is very interested in your future behavior. Any more missteps and we will not be so lenient."

Erich nodded. On one hand, he was relieved that Axel's verdict was in his favor, but on the other, fuck that guy. The way he strutted around like he was an elder annoyed him. That asshole was the same age as Adam.

There wasn't anything more to say. The verdict had been reached and Erich was a free man. As they walked back to their cars, Erich only had one thing on his mind. Sadie. He didn't like the way things had ended last night. Something was wrong and he needed to fix it, not only for her sake, but for his, as well.

CHAPTER 28

*U*sing a standard stride, it took exactly twenty-two steps to walk across her living room and back. Thirty-six if you include the dining room, though the space sat at a forty-five degree angle, causing one to turn a bit to continue pacing. If one wanted to be pedantic about it, the dining room would be considered its own entity instead of being lumped with the living room.

Sadie sighed. Those were the type of things that tended to run through her mind when she was avoiding her real-life problems. She plopped onto the Great Big Boil and let her body sink into the cushions. The muscles around her spine cracked and popped as she relaxed against the soft pillows. She let out an involuntary sigh of relief. Maybe Lauren was right about this thing. If you let your body completely relax and submit to the cushions, it did feel like a big hug.

She was doing it again. Distracting her mind with small things that didn't matter. Erich's face flashed in her memory. Judging by his expression when she had left, he had known something was wrong. She had tried to play it off, but for some reason, when she was around him, her ability to be stoic was nonexistent.

Squawking chickens interrupted her thoughts. Sadie grinned. Lauren had changed Sadie's ringtone days ago with the hope that a random text would occur during a meeting and embarrass her. Her sister had literally fallen on the floor laughing at the possibility. Sadie had kept the ring tone because the memory of it made her smile.

My car won't start. Can you come get me? I'm scared.

Sadie straightened and immediately called Lauren on her cell phone. When she didn't answer, she texted her back.

Where are you? Why won't you answer your phone?

Sadie waited impatiently, staring at her phone as if willing her sister to respond.

733 Prosperity Lane

That's it. Just an address. Sadie called her sister again, but it immediately went to voicemail. Worry gnawed at her stomach. Something was off. It was strange for Lauren to be so abrupt and mysterious. At any other time, Lauren would have called and would have been wailing into the phone about her bad luck. It had taken many tubs of Rocky Road ice cream and snickerdoodle cookies to help Lauren get over the cancellation of her favorite TV show. To say she was a drama queen was an understatement.

Sadie chewed at her lower lip as she weighed her options. With the bloodborne out there, it probably wasn't a good idea to go out on her own. She called Erich but it also went straight to voicemail. She left a quick message and tossed her phone into her purse.

Even though the bloodborne were still out there, she was not going to leave her sister stranded. Acting on impulse, she walked into her bedroom, pulled Jacki's Mti blade from her drawer, and fastened the leather band around her waist underneath her shirt. She didn't know how to fight, but she felt better having it with her. Gathering her keys, she headed toward the elevators.

Erich and the rest of Odinshield were at their meeting, but Stefen would come with her. He rarely left the building. His lack of control over his rage usually meant he was left behind. His presence could potentially create a whole other mess, but even a wild berserker by her side was better than nothing.

When he didn't answer her knock, she used her watch to gain access to his office. A quick peek revealed towers of boxes and computer equipment, but no sandy-haired berserker. She dug her phone out of her purse and called his number. Straight to voicemail. Damn, he must have gone to the meeting as well.

Cursing her bad luck, she checked the charge on her stun gun as she headed to her car. She eyed Erich's truck sitting across the parking lot. Why did this have to happen now? Perhaps it would be best if she waited until Erich returned so that he could go with her. Sadie checked her phone. Nothing from Lauren. She started her car.

On her way to 733 Prosperity Lane, Sadie once again called Erich and Lauren's cell phone. Both went to voicemail. The worry twisted her gut as she drove further into the city. Triton City was a bustling mid-sized metropolis, but it also had its seedy areas. Judging from the number of broken windows and graffiti-covered walls, Sadie could only assume that Prosperity Lane was the opposite of its name.

As she neared the address, she scanned the road for Lauren's bright green car. The city was empty, as if even the riffraff hesitated to walk its streets. Abandoned buildings butted against the cracked sidewalks and the streets were littered with trash. Sadie's intuition was screaming alarm bells. Why would Lauren be on this side of town? What had she gotten herself into?

Sadie slowly pulled up to a stoplight, her eyes darting from left to right as she took in her surroundings. Movement to her right made her jump. She giggled nervously as a white plastic bag floated along with the wind next to her window. The light turned green and her tires made a squealing sound as she accelerated.

Even though it was the middle of the day, the looming buildings cast a dark shadow upon the street, making it feel even more ominous. She was just about to turn around and speed out of there when she spotted her sister's car parked in front of what looked like an abandoned restaurant.

Heart pounding, she pulled next to the car and peered into the dark interior. She could just make out someone in the driver's seat.

"Lauren!" Sadie slammed her car in park and ran to the driver's side of Lauren's car. Her sister's head was laid on the steering wheel, her brown hair was wild like a messy cloud around her head. Sadie pulled on the door handle but the door was locked.

"Lauren," she called knocking on the window. Lauren shifted, as if woken from a deep sleep. "Lauren, it's Sadie. Open the door, sweetie."

Lauren began to straighten. She lifted her hand and brushed her hair out of her face. Sadie gasped and backed away from the window, her hand going to her stun gun. A strange woman smiled at her. She was as young as Lauren, but her skeletal frame made her look older and worn out. She rolled her window down and motioned for Sadie to come close. Sadie continued to back away.

"Where is my sister," she demanded.

The woman's smile widened, her lips stretching out into a grotesque display of teeth and gums. "All hail the Seed."

CHAPTER 29

*W*hen Erich reached Adam's car, he immediately checked his phone. His heart flipped when he saw that he had two missed calls and one voicemail from Sadie.

"Hey, I gotta stop somewhere on the way back," Adam said. Erich gave him a distracted nod as he put the phone to his ear.

"Take me downtown," Erich said, hitting the call back button. Adam gave him a quizzical look.

"What's wrong?"

Erich cursed as his call went to Sadie's voicemail. He held his phone between them and pushed the play button.

"Hi, Erich, it's Sadie. Um…Lauren's car broke down and I need to go pick her up. It's probably nothing, but I just wanted to let you know where I'm going. 733 Prosperity Lane."

Adam cursed as he swung a U-turn and started speeding in the opposite direction. It wasn't long before his phone rang. Adam answered it through his bluetooth connection.

"What's up," he said.

"Adam, what's going on?" Wade said. "We saw you shoot by us like the building was on fire."

"Lauren's car broke down," Erich said. "Sadie went downtown by herself to go pick her up."

"What's the address?" Erich told him, his voice distracted as he typed out a text message to Sadie.

"We'll meet you there," Wade said.

"No," Adam said. "Go back to headquarters and let us know if she shows up."

"Got it." Wade ended the connection.

"Don't worry, brother," Adam said. "It's probably nothing."

Erich could feel the familiar tingle in his spine. His beast was waking up. He took a couple of deep breathes to calm himself down.

"Maybe. Or the Frelshednar found a way to lure her out."

Adam snorted. "Don't let Axel get into your head. The Frelshednar don't know their ass from a hole in the ground."

Erich wasn't so sure. Luring his woman outside of the protection of Odinshield seemed exactly like something his enemy would do.

As the lush forests outside of Triton City turned into the concrete jungle of buildings and traffic, Adam fielded multiple calls. Wade reported that neither Sadie nor Lauren were at Odinshield. Brandt called demanding to know the last known location of Lauren's car. And Stefen called to report that the security cameras around the building hadn't picked up anything abnormal.

"When did she leave?" Adam asked.

"She left at 1634," Stefen said. "Lauren had left at 0815."

"Go ahead and see if there are any cameras on Prosperity Lane, just in case this is more than a flat tire."

"On it."

Erich tried Sadie's phone again and cursed as her voice-mail picked up.

"Don't worry about it, brother," Adam said. "She's probably hanging somewhere with Lauren as we speak."

Erich didn't respond, the cocktail of fear and rage causing a painful lump in his throat. Put him in front of a pack of rabid shifters and he wouldn't blink an eye. But keep him from being able to get in touch with his boratai and suddenly he was spiraling into a useless, emotional wimp.

Erich was thankful for his brother's calm demeanor because he was about to lose his shit. It was like they were kids again, with Erich being the emotional, wild one and Adam filling the protector role. He had always been that way, ever since childhood. Even before training as an Ulfhednar, he had always had a calm, serious demeanor.

Erich, on the other hand, tended to be impulsive and carefree, an easy thing when there was always his big brother to look out for him.

He straightened in his seat when Adam turned onto Prosperity Lane. He scanned both sides of the street in search of Lauren's green coupe or Sadie's blue sedan.

"I don't see them." He hated how strangled his voice sounded. Adam pretended not to notice.

"Call Wade and see if they're back home."

Erich found his friend in his contacts and hit the call button. Wade answered on the first ring.

"Nothing here," he said. "Neither Lauren or Sadie are answering their phones. Stefen tracked both of their phones and their last location was Prosperity Lane."

Erich cursed. "Let me know the second she shows up."

"Will do," Wade said. "Hey, just a heads up. Brandt is heading over there."

Erich glanced at Adam who just shrugged. "Really, why?"

"I don't know. He just took off after you."

"Okay, thanks, man."

"Brandt's on his way," Erich told his brother after he had hung up.

"Yeah, I heard. That's probably a good thing. We can cover more ground."

Brandt caught up to them on the corner of Prosperity Lane and Main Street. He followed them into a decrepit parking lot of an abandoned grocery store.

"What do you know so far?" he asked, taking off his helmet.

"Absolutely nothing," Erich said, kicking at a bag of trash on the ground. "It's like she's disappeared."

"Calm down," Adam ordered. "We don't know anything yet. They could both be hanging out somewhere and totally fine. Call them again."

Erich forced himself to unclench his fists, but he couldn't do anything about the pounding of his heart. Call them again? Why? It was pointless. Still, there was a small flicker of hope that maybe this one last time, she would answer and be totally fine. She'd tease him about worrying about her and they'd have a good laugh about it. Then he'd lock her in his room and never let her out of his sight. He pulled out his phone and hit redial.

Straight to voicemail.

His back jerked as an icy bolt of lightning shot down his spine. His vision dimmed and then brightened, every detail became enhanced. With a roar, he crushed his phone in his hand and threw it against the brick wall of the grocery store. His chieftain was on him in a heartbeat. Erich snarled as Adam held him against the brick with his forearm.

"Cool it, brother," he said. Erich's teeth ached as he clenched his jaw. If it had been anyone else holding him, Erich would have torn the fucker apart. But some part of him recognized Adam's authority.

Deep in the foggy part of his mind, he heard a soft ringing.

"That's Lauren's phone," Brandt said, his phone to his ear. He took off in a sprint. Adam released Erich, and they ran after him. They found the source of the ringing in the gutter in front of an empty apartment building. Lauren's yellow phone case peaked out from underneath a bunch of leaves. Brandt picked it up and stared at it.

"That's not good," Adam said with a curse.

That was an understatement.

They jumped as the shrill ring of Adam's cell cut through the air. Adam answered with the speakerphone.

"What?"

Stefen's voice crackled through the small speaker. "Hey, you might want to head back. I think we have something."

CHAPTER 30

"*N*o drugs. Her body needs to be pure."

Sadie slowly blinked her eyes awake. The room was dark, only the flickering flames from the fireplace giving off any light. Despite the fire, there was a chill in the air. Sadie swallowed hard, her throat feeling dry and scratchy. Movement caught her eye and she attempted to shift her body. Sharp pains in her shoulders told her that her hands were bound behind her back. For a moment, she panicked at being restrained and fought against the restraints.

"No, no, child," a deep voice crooned. "Do not struggle. You will mark up your body and that won't do."

Sadie's father appeared in her line of sight as he squatted next to the pallet of dusty blankets she was lying on.

"Father," Sadie said, her voice thick and raspy. Her father smiled. "Father, don't do this."

"You were the Seed of Light," her father whispered. "This is meant to be." He patted her arm, his eyes bright with emotion and his words coming out in a rush. "This is your destiny. And after tonight, you will be the Vessel of Light.

You will bring a new generation of pure-blooded alara. Your children will bring us into the Era of Light! Sabien be praised!"

"Sabien be praised," a chorus of voices repeated. It was then that she noticed the other people in the room, bustling about and lighting candles around the altar.

Sadie pulled against the ties that bound her wrists behind her. Her father watched her, his face impassive. As a child, her father had seemed larger than life. His wisdom and charisma had led the Children of Light through decades of growth. She had been so proud as she had watched him lead his flock toward their eventual paradise.

Watching him now, she realized that the man she had once idolized was actually weak. His mind was blank and empty.

He was just as much a tool for Sabien's use as she had been.

A woman tapped her father on his shoulder. "We are ready, priest."

Her father gave her a warm smile and nodded. "It is time for the Seed to bloom into the Vessel."

"All hail the Seed," the group murmured.

Two members pulled Sadie into a sitting position and lifted her to her feet. Sadie gritted her teeth as pinpricks of pain shot through her legs. The new position allowed her a better view of the room and her heart sank as she took in the peeling wallpaper and dilapidated building. Dirt and dried leaves, undoubtedly blown in by the multiple holes in the wall, littered the wooden floor. She was in some sort of cabin that had been long abandoned.

"Where are we? Where's Lauren?"

Her questions were met with silence as her captors dragged her to a chair in the center of the room. With a swift move, they cut the ties at her wrist and forced her into the wooden seat. Seeing her chance, she yanked her right arm out of the grip of the small woman holding her and pushed herself out of the chair.

The man holding her other arm tightened his grip. No amount of fighting could loosen it, but one free hand was all she needed. Her stun gun was gone, so she reached under her shirt and pulled her knife out of its sheath. With a hoarse yell, she swiped at the man holding her. The man's eyes widened in surprise. He hissed as the blade sliced his forearm.

"Let me go," Sadie screamed, whipping the knife through the air in a frenzy. She may not have any fighting skills, but the knife at least put her on equal footing. Or so she thought.

One small dagger was no match for a group of crazed cult members willing to die for their cause. She screamed as three of them wrestled the knife out of her hand. Restraining her arms, they looked at her father for direction. He approached slowly, holding his hands up in a sign of peace.

"Shhhh...now now, you don't want to fight us," her father said, his voice soft like he was soothing a wild animal.

Sadie kicked at him, grinning in satisfaction as her foot connected with flesh. Her father grunted and turned hurt eyes toward her.

"Sadie, we're not going to hurt you, we're trying to help—"

"Get her in the chair!" At the order, more Children of Light came over and they roughly forced her back into the chair. She screamed and pushed against them, but their numbers were too high and she was starting to tire. As each limb was forced against the chair, they tied her to it with zip ties. During the struggle, her father had turned around and bowed low to the man who had entered the room.

"My lord," he said.

The man ignored him and approached Sadie's chair. As

he approached, the Children of Light shrunk away, bowing low at the waist.

"Sadie Carmichael. We meet at last."

Sadie stared at the man. He seemed familiar but she couldn't place him. He was handsome and young, with dark eyes and a thick head of black hair that curled charmingly at the ends.

He seemed to notice her confusion and chuckled. "I guess Lauren never talked about me. I'm offended."

At the mention of Lauren, the pieces began to fall into place. She had seen him before. Lauren had gushed over photos of them together.

"Zane," she whispered.

Zane flashed her a charming smile. "So she has spoken of me. I'm pleased that I made such an impression upon her."

"Where is she," Sadie demanded.

Zane stared at her, his head slightly tilted. "My sweet Lauren should be the least of your worries," he said. "Your parents have told me great things about you. About the powerful alara who had escaped their grasp. We've been looking for you."

"Why?"

"To provide sustenance, of course. With every new blood-borne I create and every time we feed, Sabien gains power. And as he gains power, the bloodborne become stronger. Your blood and your womb, will propel us into a new era."

"Sabien be praised," the Children of Light murmured. Sadie had forgotten they were even in the room. They all watched her with rapturous expressions.

Sadie couldn't control her shivering. "Sabien is not real," she said through gritted teeth.

Zane chuckled. "Fortunately for us all, his eventual release does not require your belief in him."

"It would be better for everyone if you submit to him,

daughter," her father said. "As his vessel, you will prove quite instrumental in Sabien's release. If you do this, we will all be transformed into a bloodborne and will have the strength to prepare the world for Sabien's return."

"Sabien be praised," the Children murmured.

Zane closed his eyes and smelled the air. "It's been days since I've fed properly. Humans. Functional but not really fulfilling." He opened his eyes and looked at her, his irises rimmed in red. The flickering light from the fireplace caused dark shadows to dance across his face, giving him a feverish, demonic look. Sadie shrank back against her chair.

"Perhaps we could drain a little from her and you can partake from the holy bowl. Sabien will not like his vessel to be marked," her father said, his hands folded in a gesture of supplication.

Zane considered it. "No. I like it fresh from the tap, as they say."

Her father looked worried. "It's just…my lord…with the others, the alara didn't survive the feeding…and she is our next vessel."

Zane bent over and put his face close to hers. He seemed to be smelling her skin as he gently rubbed his cheek against hers. Slowly, he pressed his lips against her jawline. Sadie pulled away, but he gripped the other side of her face in a painful grip and held her in place. Nausea bubbled up in Sadie's stomach and she swallowed compulsively to keep herself from throwing up.

"No," Sadie said, her voice shaky and weak. She turned her eyes to her father, who stood behind Zane, wringing his hands and looking worried. There would be no help from him.

Sadie froze as Zane ran his teeth against the skin of her neck. He released the hold on her face and grabbed her shoulders. Her mind flashed to the bodies in the morgue, their skin cold and their throats ripped out.

"No…I…You don't have to do th—" Sadie cried out as razor-sharp pins pierced her neck. Zane replaced his teeth with his lips. He moaned as his mouth moved against her neck, rhythmically sucking at the holes that he had created. His hands caressed her shoulders like a lover soothing a nervous virgin. Sadie pulled against her restraints but was helpless.

Her father fluttered nearby, wringing his hands and looking worried. "Sire, she needs her strength. She is to be the vessel."

With a reluctant grunt, Zane released her neck. He staggered back a few steps, his eyes red and his face soft and dreamy. As soon as he had stepped away, Sadie's father closed in and pressed a cloth to her neck. She hardly noticed, all of her attention and hatred focused on the man who had by then collapsed against the wall.

"Don't worry about him," her father said. "He always gets like that after feeding from an alara. He'll recover in a few minutes."

Sadie stared at her father in disbelief. "I don't give a shit about him. I hope he dies," she hissed. Her father's eyes widened and he flapped his hands in front of her, making a shushing sound.

"You must not upset the master," he said, but Sadie wasn't listening. All of her attention was on the dark silhouette in the doorway, his glowing golden eyes locked right on her.

lood.
Flesh.

She sat in the middle of the room, her eyes wide and her neck red. Blood. The beast sniffed the air. His boratai, humans, and something else. A creature.

The humans went down easily, putting up little fight as they tried to come between him and his boratai.

He was at her side in an instant. With a few flicks of his fingers, he broke the plastic strips that were securing her to the chair. She was afraid, he could smell it.

He heard the creature before he saw it. A soft scrape upon the wooden floor. The scent of his boratai's blood rode upon the gust of air created by its approach. The beast straightened, spun, and shot out an arm. The creature dodged and moved away. It was fast. Faster than the beast.

The beast roared. The creature stopped. It spoke. His boratai's blood was upon its breath. The beast snarled. The creature came at him, slashing him across the arm. He ignored it, for the beast did not feel pain, only rage.

The creature crouched against the wall. It leapt at him. It

ripped at the beast's face and neck with its nails. It said words.

The beast grabbed its arm. The creature hissed. His boratai's blood was upon its breath. With a roar, the beast twisted his body and brought the creature's arm down upon his knee. The sound of bones breaking filled the air. The creature screamed. The beast smiled.

The creature lashed out at him. The beast smelled fresh blood. His blood, not his boratai's. He will protect her. With a roar, the beast threw the creature against the wall. The creature crumpled to the ground.

A noise behind him. The beast sniffed the air as he scanned the room. More men have arrived. Half men, half beasts. Brothers. The creature saw them too. It paused for a second. The beast lashed out, punching it in the jaw. The creature slammed against the wall but jumped immediately to its feet.

Two knives whistled through the air and lodged into the creature's chest. It opened its mouth and hissed, long fangs extending outside of its jaw. His boratai's blood was upon its breath. The beast growled.

A brother launched himself at the thing, his limbs almost invisible as he landed a flurry of blows upon the thing. It went down. More knives whistled through the air and impaled themselves into the wooden floor. A miss.

The creature had shifted away and was getting back onto its feet. The beast ran toward it, but the creature turned and sprinted toward the window. The glass shattered with the impact of its body as it disappeared out of the window. Two of his brothers followed. The beast ran to the window. He must kill it.

A soft noise. A woman. His woman. His boratai. Afraid. Bloody. The beast spun away from the window. He went to her. He needed her. He would protect her.

A man stepped in his way. Human. Holding a needle up as if to stab him with it.

The man said words. He trembled. He was afraid. The beast grinned.

The man was in his way. The beast needed his boratai. She was bloody. He would protect her.

He grabbed the man by his throat and squeezed.

"No, Erich! Stop!"

The beast froze. His boratai. The man struggled. He gripped the beast's wrist. His boratai was next to him. Holding his arm. She was bloody. The beast snarled. The man must die.

"No, Erich! Look at me!"

The beast looked at her. His heart pounded at the sight of her. His boratai. The beast smiled. His boratai looked scared. The beast frowned.

"Let him go."

The beast released the man. His boratai wet her lips. The beast watched the pink tongue as it peaked out of her mouth. The beast smiled. He must fuck her. His boratai put her hands on his face.

"Look at me."

The beast looked at her. His boratai. He grabbed her waist and pulled her against him. He kissed her, his hands snaking down to explore her body. She pushed against his chest. He stepped back. His boratai looked frightened. The beast snarled. He would protect her. His boratai cupped his face with her hands.

"Come back to me, Erich. Come back to me."

Erich blinked. Sadie was holding his head and staring at him. His eyes dropped to her neck. Blood. What the fuck?

"Sadie, baby, are you okay?"

She watched him with tearful eyes and didn't answer. What the fuck just happened? Erich pulled her toward him.

She fell against his chest, releasing big body-racking sobs. He surveyed the room. Bodies lay scattered about. Candles were lit. His eyes stopped on a wooden chair and narrowed.

"We good, brother?"

Adam. His brother. His chieftain. He approached slowly, watching him warily.

"I'm good," Erich said. "What the fuck is going on?"

"Stefen tracked Sadie's watch to this cabin right outside of town."

"I remember," Erich said. "But things get a little fuzzy after that. I guess I went nuclear."

Adam nodded, his eyes going to Sadie, assessing the situation. He scanned the room. "You went nuclear as soon as we pulled up. It was stupid of you to go in with no backup, but I don't blame you. This whole situation is fucked up."

That was an understatement. Eventually, he was going to need to find out why Sadie was in a shitty cabin with blood down her shirt, but for now, he would enjoy the fact that she was safe in his arms.

"Where are the others?"

"Wade and Ty went after the bloodborne. I don't know where Brandt is," Adam said, his face suddenly looking tired. "Come on, let's get the hell out of here."

"No," a small voice cried out. A tall, gaunt man was crouched in the corner, his hands held out in front of him in supplication. "You must not take her from us. We can't lose her again. She is our vessel. She will bring about the rise of Sabien."

Erich tried to pull Sadie behind him, but she held on to him. "No, Erich, don't hurt him."

Erich looked at her in disbelief. "Is this the man that hurt you?"

Sadie shook her head. "No...not really. I mean...I don't know. He's my father."

She looked so confused and vulnerable that Erich pulled her closer, not at all minding the death grip that she had on his waist. He locked eyes with Adam.

With a nod, Adam grabbed the man and pulled him to his feet. He half dragged Sadie's father to the door. Sadie didn't seem to notice. Her sobs had quieted to small sniffles.

Erich stroked her hair. "Sadie, don't be afraid. I'm here now and I will never leave your side again."

She pulled back and looked at him with wet eyes. "I don't think you can make that kind of promise, Erich," she said with a small smile. "It's not practical."

Erich ran a thumb along her cheek, erasing the line that her tears had made and wishing he could erase the cause.

"You have no idea how wrong you are, baby," he said, his voice soft yet firm. "As of today, I will be moving into your apartment. And if you get tired of me, I will sleep in the fucking hallway outside of your door. You will never be without my protection again."

Fresh tears welled up in her eyes and he silently cursed himself for being the cause. "That was supposed to reassure you."

She wiped at her tears and sniffed. "It did," she said. "I'm sorry. I don't know why I'm crying."

"Never apologize for how you feel." Erich cupped her cheek and gently brushed his lips against hers. "I love you, baby. You are my boratai. Until the day I die, you will own me one hundred percent. And nothing like this will ever happen again. Even if there's another Thing, you will be right by my side, I don't give a shit what tradition says."

Fresh tears welled in her eyes as she gave him a watery smile. With a sigh, she tucked herself under his arm as if seeking his warmth. Considering the carnage around them, it was probably best to get her out of there.

Erich led her out of the cabin and toward the side road

where they had hidden their vehicles. Adam had put her father in the back of one of Odinshield's SUVs. Sadie gasped as the door to the other SUV opened and her sister burst out of it. With a sob of relief, she let go of Erich and embraced her sister, the two women crying into each other's shoulders.

While the women had their reunion, Erich scanned the surrounding trees. Sadie's neck wound told him that there had been a bloodborne present. Judging by the fact that all of the bodies in the cabin were human, the bloodborne bastard was still out there, and with his beastly adrenaline leaving his body, the post-nuclear weakness was already starting to set in.

He draped an arm around both women. "Let's get you inside. We'll be heading home in a few."

They didn't argue and he soon had them safe inside the SUV. He stood outside, scanning the trees around them. A soft whistle drew his attention to his right. Adam and Brandt approached, both of them sheathing long blades into their waist holsters.

"Perimeter's secure," Brandt said, his pale eyes scanning the surrounding trees. His gaze flicked to the SUV's interior before looking away.

Adam said. "You two, take the girls back to Odinshield. I'll follow when Wade and Ty get back."

He didn't have to tell him twice. Erich was itching to get Sadie out of there and safe within Odinshield's walls. Now that the immediate danger was over, he wanted to gather her in his arms and never let go, but he resisted the urge to sit in the back with Sadie. He had a job to do and his current mission was to get the girls home. They were soon on the road and speeding in the direction of Odinshield.

CHAPTER 32

The Seed of Light tucked a stray lock of her dark hair under her white veil. Covered from head to toe in white linen, she sat on the hard wooden bench, not moving a muscle as she prepared to give her offering to Sabien, Keeper of the Holy Blood. She took a deep breath and released it slowly, allowing her muscles to gently relax. Her hands fell open, palms up, as they rested on her knees. Someone held a small glass in front of her mouth. She tilted her head and allowed the thick liquid to coat her tongue before swallowing. Her body slumped against the wall, her mind developing a delicious fogginess. She thought of Sabien. Her lord. Her protector. Her heart swelled as she thought of the offering she was about to give to him.

"It is time, child." Her father lifted her off of the bench.

Sadie jerked awake with a sharp cry. Almost immediately, a strong hand stroked her arm. Sadie allowed herself to relax as the deep, masculine voice murmured soothing words. After three months, it had almost become a ritual.

True to his word, Erich had moved into the apartment she shared with Lauren. After spending the first few nights on the Great Big Boil, she had taken pity on him and invited him to share her room. It had turned out to be exactly what she needed. As it turned out, the perfect balm to her night-mares was a soft, sleepy word from her berserker. She still had the nightmares, of course, but with Erich by her side, they didn't last long.

Sadie gently moved the blanket off of her and sat up. She took a second to watch her boyfriend, his face smooth and youthful in sleep. His eyes snapped open as she stood.

"What's wrong," he asked, his voice was thick from sleep but his eyes were fully alert.

Sadie moved the thick comforter back in place. "Nothing, everything's fine. Go back to sleep."

He closed his eyes and within moments he was breathing the rhythmic breathing of someone in deep sleep. Sadie shook her head. It was amazing how he could fall asleep within seconds.

Putting on her robe and slippers, she padded out into the main living area. Lauren was already awake and sipping on a cup of coffee. Her coloring had slowly returned now that her boyfriend wasn't taking small sips of her blood without her knowledge. Hypnosis. Yet another skill that the bloodborne possessed. Stefen had been thrilled when he had learned that they were capable of entrancing humans.

She gave Sadie a weak smile as she entered the kitchen. Even though it had been months, they were both going to have to work through what had been done to them.

Sadie pushed one of Eric's paperbacks to the side and joined her sister at the table. "Are you packed?"

Lauren nodded. "I'm still not sure this is a good idea."

"We can't stay in here forever. We have to get out and move on with our lives," Sadie said.

"Easy for you to say," Lauren said with a frown. "You have Erich watching over you twenty-four seven. I have no one.

The man I thought I loved turned out to be some blood-sucking psycho."

Sadie reached across the table and grabbed Lauren's hand. "You are not alone. You have me and every single berserker at Odinshield. With Erich and Ty escorting us to the Academy, we will be well protected."

Lauren didn't look convinced. "I don't see why I have to go. You're the doctor. You can tell the Intellects everything they need to know."

"They have limited knowledge about the bloodborne. You were close to Zane. You may have picked up on something and not even realized it. Besides, it's good for you to get out of this apartment. We both need to get out and rejoin society."

Sadie's stomach twisted as Lauren's normally vibrant brown eyes dropped to stare at her hands. While Sadie had gone through a traumatic event, so had Lauren. She was dealing with the betrayal of a loved one who had kidnapped her, tied her up, and dumped her in the forest. If Brandt hadn't found her, Sadie didn't know what she would have done. She tapped Lauren's hand.

"Brighten up. Maybe all of that cold air will help us."

Lauren rolled her eyes. "Ugh. Don't remind me."

"Pack your coat," Sadie said as she scooted back her chair. "And your boots."

Sadie chuckled as Lauren's exaggerated groan followed behind her.

Erich was in the shower when she stepped into her room. She sat on her bed and watched as he ran the soap over the muscles of his body. Enjoying the lusty heat that spread from within her, she raked her eyes back up his strong legs, ripped abs, and muscular chest. She jumped in surprise when she found two blue eyes staring back at her, his mouth twisted in a smirk.

"Take a picture, it'll last longer," he said.

Feeling the heat on her cheeks, she looked away and busied herself with making the bed. "I was just wondering how long you're going to take," she said, her voice sounding snappier than she'd like.

Erich chuckled. "Don't be shy, come join me. We'll save time. The sooner we're dressed, the sooner we can hit the road."

Sadie glanced at Erich. Her man. Her boratai. At first, she had thought that being his boratai meant he was using or possessing her. That the only value she had was the calm that her presence, her body, gave him. In reality, it was the opposite. Her stomach fluttered at the thought of such a handsome man belonging to her, body and soul.

With a small sigh, she pulled on the belt of her robe. "I guess you're right. We need to meet Ty downstairs in fifteen minutes."

Erich grinned as she took off her nightdress and stepped into the shower. They ended up being very late.

"Let's go, princess," Ty said as he took Lauren's suitcase from her hand. "Damn, girl, what do you have in here? We're only going to be gone for three weeks."

Lauren rolled her eyes as Ty lifted her bag into the back of the SUV with an exaggerated grunt. "If you can't lift a little suitcase, I can get my sister to do it."

Ty pretended to assess Sadie with a critical eye. "Nah, I think I can take her," he said.

Wade and Erich approached the SUV with Stefen talking to them in an animated manner. "And don't forget to meet with the headmaster to discuss the disparate properties of elemental magic between generations. They've touched on it a little but they are obviously missing a piece of the puzzle."

"Yeah, I'll mention it," Erich said, absentmindedly. He glanced at Sadie and winked at her. "We ready to go?"

"Yep, load 'em up," Ty said. He rapped his knuckles onto the top of the SUV. "Stefen, move out of the way. Erich will be sure to mention your nerd shit."

Chuckling, Wade pulled Stefen back so that Erich could open the driver's side door.

"I'll email the details to you, just in case," Stefen said.

"Good, do that," Erich said.

Sadie watched Stefen's crestfallen face as Erich pulled away from the curb. It was unfortunate that he couldn't come, but rules were rules. The Academy refused to overturn his banishment, despite his in-depth research of the bloodborne.

The warm feeling of Erich's palm against her hand distracted her from her rather sad thoughts. He looked over at her and gave her hand a squeeze.

She smiled, enjoying the warm spread in her chest. Her boratai. Soul mate. Lover. Whatever you wanted to call it. Her man had risked his life to save hers, and if that wasn't love, she didn't know what was.

EPILOGUE

*S*abien, Render of Flesh, Keeper of the Holy Blood, shuddered within his cell. He placed a finger on the spider webbed wall of his prison and sighed as the power from his followers seeped through the cracks and into his skin. He had felt the first crack a thousand or so years ago. It was hard to tell. Time ran differently in his prison. Only one thing could have cracked his cell: an elemental stone had been destroyed. That one crack had continued to splinter as his followers had awoken. He had watched each one form. Felt his followers' power as they had fed and created more bloodborne. His priest had been busy.

He pressed against the splintered crystal and allowed his essence to seep through the cracks. As his followers fed, they made him stronger. As his strength increased, his essence made them stronger. He smiled. Soon he'll be powerful enough to shatter his prison, and the seven nations will wish they had never crossed him.

Enjoy this book? Please leave a review.

Hey there, lovely readers!

I'm so excited that you've joined me on this journey through the world of paranormal romance. Your thoughts and reviews mean the absolute world to me. Whether you fell in love with the characters, got lost in the action, or just had a blast, please take a moment to share your thoughts in a review. Your words have the power to make this author's heart sing and help others discover the magic in my books. I'm beyond grateful for your support and can't wait to keep sharing more enchanting tales with you.

With heaps of appreciation and bookish love,

Avery Haynes

ACKNOWLEDGMENTS

I have always been a daydreamer, especially as a child, and putting one of my mental adventures into a novel has been a dream come true. This never would have happened without the love and support of my friends and family.

I must first thank my mother, who instilled the love of reading in me. Thank you for the pep talks and endless amount of support.

My husband and partner in crime, Kevin. Thank you for being my sounding board and my inspiration.

Jasmin and Liz, thank you for your invaluable advice during my rough draft. Yes, you're right, Jasmin. Alpha males don't look through peepholes. I've kept that in mind in all of my writing.

My kiddos, who listened politely as I rambled on about characters and storylines they knew nothing about.

And thank you to my friends and family who read my book and cheered me on throughout the process. Your support means so much to me.

ABOUT THE AUTHOR

Avery Haynes loves movies, crafting, and losing herself in a good book. On the weekends, you can find her playing video games with her kids or strolling through the aisles of a craft store. You can follow her on TikTok (@Averysfiction), Instagram (@Averysfiction) and Facebook (Averysfiction)

Join her newsletter to stay up to date on beta read requests and book announcements.

http://www.averyhaynes.com

ALSO BY AVERY HAYNES

Ancient Elements Series

The Shadow of Fire

Odinshield Berserkers

Warrior Awakened

Warrior's Salvation

Warrior's Redemption

What happens when a berserker known for his strict control meets his soul mate?

Adam Birkeland, CEO of Odinshield Protection Agency, has spent a lifetime being the perfect soldier that the Odinshield needs. But a desperate call from his brother shatters his controlled existence, and as he looks into Nia's eyes for the first time, he is overcome with one thought: Mine.

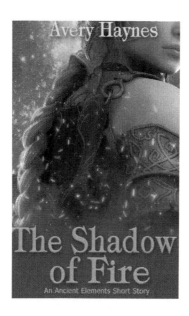

A heart pounding introduction to the Ancient Elements universe

Nadia Inavov is a fledgling elemental, only recently coming into her power. After an attack on her camp, she must flee from the mighty empire that seeks to steal her magic. With the other elementals dead, nature will find new hosts, women worthy of wielding the power of the elements. It is Nadia's duty to seek them out so the balance can be restored. But first, she must survive the night.

This is a short story set within the Ancient Elements universe. It's a quick read at 1.5k words.

Made in the USA
Columbia, SC
19 March 2024